MARVIN AND THE MOTHS

MARVIN AND THE MOTHS

Matthew Holm & Jonathan Follett

with illustrations by Matthew Holm

SCHOLASTIC PRESS • NEW YORK

Library of Congress Cataloging-in-Publication Data available

ISBN 978-0-545-87674-2

10 9 8 7 6 5 4 3 2 1   16 17 18 19 20

Printed in the U.S.A.   23

First edition, October 2016

Book design by Christopher Stengel

To Cyndi and Jen

1

The Foundation of a Successful Life

Marvin Watson stared at the thirty feet of rope hanging from the steel beams of the ceiling and wondered what scheduling god he had offended to get gym as his very first class of the year. When he got up that morning, Marvin's two biggest concerns were making sure he didn't wear anything funny-looking and that he didn't do anything to embarrass himself on his first day of middle school. Here, fifteen minutes after entering the building, was the opportunity to do both.

"What's the matter, couldn't afford a new uniform?" asked Marvin's cousin, Little Stevie Upton. Marvin's gym shorts from the previous year were riding a little high, and his T-shirt had the words "GO PIGLETS!" above the face of a shy little piggy, which was the mascot of Butcherville Elementary School. Everyone else was wearing new red-and-gold gym uniforms that featured the emblem of the Crashing Boar, which was the middle school's symbol. Little Stevie had even accented his uniform with a custom-made gold-trimmed tracksuit with his name monogrammed across the chest. The gold trim may have been actual gold, and it appeared that the large boar logo on the back of the jacket had diamonds for eyes.

"This track suit costs more than your house, Watson," Little Stevie said. "And it probably smells better." Marvin was used to his cousin, Stevie, tormenting him at family functions, but being tormented by him at school was a new experience. Until this year, Little Stevie had attended Swineheart Academy, a private elementary school.

"My mom didn't have time to take me shopping," Marvin said lamely. "You know, because of Baby Harry."

"It's been three weeks since he was born. Don't blame the kid for your problems, Watson," Stevie said.

Marvin stared down at his uniform, the bashful piglet on the T-shirt riding slightly above his belly button. The pig looked the way Marvin felt.

Pigs were big in Marvin's hometown of Butcherville. All the school sports teams were named after pigs—the

Piglets for the elementary school, the Crashing Boars for the middle school, and the Trotters for the high school. Just as a city like Atlanta is flush with streets named for peaches, many of Butcherville's roads and byways were named after cuts of pork, like swanky Loin Lane and the unfortunately titled Butt Boulevard.

It was all because Butcherville was the home of Pork Loaf International, makers of the world-renowned Pork Loaf Log Roll. Butcherville was a company town, proud of its heritage, and the type of place where the flagship product in the company's line of processed, enriched meats was often served at all three meals.

Lunch was already on Marvin's mind. He was finding it difficult to concentrate on his physical education as the smell of cooking food wafted out from the kitchen and into the cafetorium where gym class was held. As soon as class was over, the janitors would start setting up the room for lunch. Marvin was counting the minutes.

He tried to pay attention as Mr. Franco, the gym teacher, began explaining the feats of strength they would be expected to perform. "Welcome, class. In this room, over the next three years, you will make the transition from being boys to being young men. Just as Pork Loaf is the foundation of a good sandwich, physical fitness is the foundation of a successful life. Today, we'll start with some baseline fitness tests so we can gauge your progress over the year. It doesn't matter how long it takes you to climb this rope, or how many push-ups you can do, or how fast you can run a mile. It just matters that you try your very best. Now let's get to it!"

The students stood with their backs to the cold, painted cinder-block wall of the cafetorium. They had lined up by alphabetical order to take attendance, and Marvin was thankful his last name put him at the end of the line. He didn't want to have to go first.

"Let's start at . . . *that* end of the line," Mr. Franco said, and his finger slowly swung across the crowd. When it came to rest, it was pointing squarely at Marvin.

"Me?" Marvin said. "But it's the first day of school!"

"Well, then you shouldn't have anything to complain about yet, should you?" Mr. Franco said.

Marvin approached the rope like he would a thirty-foot snake. He turned to Mr. Franco. "What do I do?" he said, looking for some instruction.

"Just try to climb it with your arms first," said Mr. Franco. "If you need to use your legs, that's okay."

Marvin nodded warily. Although there had been ropes in his elementary school gym classes, climbing them hadn't been mandatory. Marvin had always preferred running, swimming—or just about anything else. So he had managed to dodge rope-climbing until now.

"I'm going to count down from five and then hit the stopwatch," said Mr. Franco. "Ready? Five, four, three, two, one—GO!" Mr. Franco pressed his thumb down with a click, and Marvin leaped at the rope, which sent him swinging out in a wide arc and back toward the line of students. Stevie, who was next in line, helpfully gave him a hard shove to send him back on his way.

Mr. Franco was beginning to look annoyed. "Come on, quit goofing around," he said. "Start climbing. Use those arms!"

"I'm using my arms to hold on!" Marvin said as he careened through the air. He couldn't figure out how to make any progress. If he let go to grab higher on the rope, he'd end up falling.

"Use your legs!" Mr. Franco said.

Marvin brought his legs together and tried to shimmy his way up the rope. He was rewarded for his efforts by the sound of tearing fabric and a collective gasp from the other students, followed by slowly rising laughter. Marvin tried to glance back over his shoulder to see how badly his shorts had ripped, but that just put him into a spin. After what seemed to Marvin like an eternity of struggling, Mr. Franco grabbed him and lowered him to the ground.

"Stop, stop, stop," Mr. Franco said. "We don't have time for this. You're taking way too long."

"I thought you said that it didn't matter how long it took," said Marvin. "Just that I try my very best."

"You can't try your best if you don't have any pants," said Mr. Franco. "But don't worry—you can stay after school sometime and make up the fitness test."

As he was contemplating the prospect of not only

doing this again, but staying after school to do it, Marvin heard Stevie call out, "Nice funderoos, Watson!"

"They're not funderoos," Marvin protested. "They're just regular underwear."

"Yes, yes," Mr. Franco said. "We can all see your big-boy underwear. Now get in the back of the line."

The back of the line was just fine by Marvin. That's where he'd wanted to be from the start, he thought to himself, as the ventilation fans at the edge of the cafetorium sent a cool breeze through his tattered gym shorts.

2

The Smelly Kid No One Liked

Marvin fared a little better in the next class, algebra. It was extremely confusing, but at least no one saw his underwear. After that came the library, where Mrs. Goudy, the librarian, greeted the class with an enthusiastic smile.

"Welcome, young explorers!" she said. "The library is a sacred space. A place where the vibrations of the past and the future overlap like ripples crossing in a pond. Here, the pursuit of knowledge is hallowed above all else. Here, all questions are valid, and we will help you take charge of your own education and find your voice."

She paused. Marvin and the other students stared blankly back.

"Now, we will begin this exploration together by exploring—silence," she said.

Marvin raised his hand. "I thought you said we were going to find our voice," he said.

Mrs. Goudy looked at him with a sour expression. Marvin could almost see her mentally jotting down his name for future use. "Your *inner* voice," she said.

"We've already seen his inner voice," a boy said from the back of the room. "When his gym shorts ripped." Laughter spread through the room.

Mrs. Goudy frowned and clapped her hands together. "Enough of that," she said. "I want you all to explore the library—while being quiet—for fifteen minutes."

"Then what?" Marvin asked.

"Then we will begin the extended lesson," Mrs. Goudy said, "where you will sit quietly for another thirty minutes. You may put your heads down if you like."

Marvin laid his head down on the table in front of him. He hadn't slept well the night before, or for about a dozen nights before that. It was nice to be able to close his eyes without having to hear a baby wail.

Forty-five minutes later, Marvin awoke to the sound of the bell ringing. His sleeve was wet with drool, and the library was empty. He grabbed his books and hurried off to the cafetorium for lunch.

Marvin's lunch period started at 11 a.m. Last year, his mom had usually packed him a nice sandwich, but this morning she'd been too busy with the baby, and had just given him lunch money. He picked up a tray and took his place in the long, slow-moving line.

As he inched forward, he kept an eye on the lunch tables. They were steadily filling up. Marvin spotted one of his classmates from elementary school, Phil Kazarian, sitting at a nearby table.

"Hey, Phil! Can you save me a seat?" Marvin said.

Phil shook his head and stretched his arms out over the still-empty benches on either side of him. "No can do, Watson. These are all spoken for."

Marvin found it odd that Phil had called him "Watson." Only Little Stevie had ever done that before. He glanced around to find someone else he recognized who might have an empty seat.

"Tilly!" he said, waving his arms. Tilly Hoefecker, who had been one of his best friends in music class, was sitting at a table with several other girls—and three open seats. Tilly and he had both played saxophone, and they had bonded over the fact that they were both equally terrible at it. She looked him up and down for a long moment, then shrugged.

"Sorry, Watson. Girl power," she said, gesturing at the all-female table.

"Oh, okay," Marvin said, halfheartedly raising his fist in the air in support of "girl power."

Now he was getting nervous. Most of the tables seemed to be at capacity, and the few he saw that still had spaces were being guarded by grim-faced students who all silently shook their heads at him. Marvin rushed through the rest of the lunch line, not even looking at what the lunch ladies slapped onto his tray, and began a frantic quest for an open seat.

After a long minute of fruitless searching, he heard a familiar voice call out, "Hey, Tarzan! Need somewhere to sit?" Marvin turned and saw Little Stevie at a nearby table with one open seat left.

"What did you call me?" Marvin asked, confused.

Next to Stevie sat Amber Bluestone, a girl Marvin knew from elementary school but had rarely spoken to. Beside the open space on the bench was Roland Offenbach, Stevie's burly enforcer. Roland never said much; even at this age, his weight had exceeded his IQ.

"Aren't you the one who was swinging from a rope in nothing but his underwear?" Amber asked with a mean smile.

"Sorry you missed the show, Amber," Marvin said. "I'm doing an encore presentation in forty-five minutes."

"What? Eww," Amber said. She turned to Stevie. "He's not really going to sit with us, is he?"

"Of course he is," Stevie said. "This is my cousin, and my dad always says that family's important."

Amber turned to Marvin. "Well, we're doing you a favor. Family or not."

Marvin set his tray on the table and sat down awkwardly. He stared at his food and began to eat.

"Nice lunch, Watson," Stevie said, pointing to the goop in the polystyrene bowls on Marvin's lunch tray. "Is that the 'Back-to-School Casserole'? Or is that the mushy peas? I'm having trouble telling the difference."

"Yeah," Roland said with a chuckle. "The difference."

"Heh heh," Marvin said, forcing a fake laugh. "Yeah, maybe they call it 'Back-to-School Casserole' because it's been sitting around since the end of last school year." He smiled. No one else did.

"Are you trying to be funny?" Amber asked.

"Is it working?" Marvin said.

"No," she said.

"I was afraid of that," Marvin said.

"Look at poor Tarzan here," Stevie said. "He needs help being funny. Let's assist him." He looked over at Roland. "What's funny, Roland?"

"Casserole in the milk is funny," Roland said. He scooped up Marvin's casserole in his bare hand and shoved it into the carton of milk on Marvin's tray.

It all happened so fast that Marvin didn't know how to react. Then Stevie said, "That *is* funny. But you know what's funnier? *Eating* the casserole in the milk."

"What?" Marvin said. "I'm not eating that."

"I'll give you a dollar if you eat it," Stevie said. Marvin looked around for some help. Amber stared back at him with glittering eyes and a half smirk.

"Maybe you could use the money for some new clothes," Amber said.

"Why would I need new clothes?" Marvin asked.

Stevie's eyes never left Marvin. "Roland?" he said.

Roland stood up and grabbed a large bowl from his own tray. It was full of sauerkraut and mini Pork Loaf sausages. "Shower-kraut!" Roland shouted, dumping the bowl over Marvin's head. The pickled cabbage and its juices ran down Marvin's face, stinging his eyes and soaking his shirt. Laughter bubbled up around the table, and echoing cries of "Shower-kraut! Shower-kraut!" rang out from the other kids.

Marvin jerked to his feet, scraping the sausages and strands of cabbage from his hair. Before he could do anything but sputter in protest, Roland said, "Now you owe me two dollars. For ruining my lunch with your head."

Amber sniffed loudly. "Ugh—you stink!" she said, pinching her nose shut. "Are we done doing your cousin a favor, Stevie?"

"Yeah, I think so," Stevie said. "You should probably leave now, Watson."

"Yeah," Marvin said. "Right." He grabbed the tray holding what was left of his lunch and staggered away from the table in shock.

Marvin wandered through the cafetorium in a fever of kraut and humiliation. He kept bumping into students who angrily shoved him off, saying, "Get away!" and, "You smell like a walking hot dog!"

Eventually the haze began to clear, and he glimpsed in the distance—like a mirage of an oasis in the desert—a table with some empty seats. As Marvin drew closer, he saw that there was, in fact, only one person sitting there.

Finally! Marvin thought. *Some good luck.*

But as he walked down the aisle toward the empty table, he noticed a smell. A strong smell—stronger even than his own perfume of sauerkraut. He wondered if the janitors had forgotten to take out the trash before the school closed for the summer. Or if maybe a mouse had died in the walls sometime in July. Or if the breeze had shifted in from the direction of the landfill.

When Marvin finally sat down and looked to his left, he realized to his dismay that the smell was coming from none of those things. The stench was emanating from his tablemate, a boy with white-blond hair named Lee Skluzacek. Lee, naturally, had been given the nickname "Smell-Lee" in elementary school.

Now Marvin understood why the table was empty.

"Hey, Marvin," Lee said. "How was your summer?"

"Um, it was okay," said Marvin. He tried breathing through his mouth instead of his nose so he wouldn't have to smell Lee's odor. "How was yours?" he gasped.

"Oh, you know," said Lee. "Same old, same old."

"Yeah," said Marvin. "I can see you haven't changed much since last year." He gulped some more air. "Um, Lee, I'm going to have to move way over here to the end of the table."

"Not a problem," Lee said cheerfully. "That's what my grandmother does at home."

Marvin slid his tray down the long table away from Lee. Once he was perched out by the aisle, the smell was only slightly swampy, but still strong enough to overwhelm the almost equally unpleasant aroma of shower-kraut. Marvin considered this a mixed blessing and tried to eat his lunch.

"So, I hear that you were swinging naked from a rope in gym class," Lee said.

Marvin glanced over. "Oh, it wasn't that bad," he said. "I was just in my underwear."

"That's still pretty bad, Marvin," Lee said.

Marvin returned to his food. He had not put more than three bites into his mouth when he heard a voice cry out, "Hey, it's the stink twins!" The voice was that of Stevie, of course. He, Roland, and Amber had finished lunch and were on their way out of the cafetorium. "I'm glad you found a friend, Watson. You guys are like two cheeks on the same butt."

"What do you want, Stevie?" Marvin said.

"Just coming by to tell you that my dad said I have to go to your lame barbecue next weekend."

"It's not mine," Marvin said. "It's for my baby brother."

"Is *that* what we're doing next Saturday?" Amber asked Stevie.

"Ooh, ooh, ooh!" Lee said from the far side of the table, waving his arm in the air. "I love barbecue!"

Amber wrinkled her nose. "Paul Thackerman would never have taken me to visit a class-D table."

"Your ex?" Stevie said with a snort. "Paul Thackerman is a public-school dork."

"Oh, don't give me that I-went-to-private-school nonsense again."

Stevie turned to Marvin. "Girl trouble. You understand."

Marvin, who had never had "girl trouble," said, "No."

"I don't understand, either," Lee called out from the end of the table.

"Big surprise," Stevie said, rolling his eyes. He turned to Marvin. "Tell your mother we're bringing a cake." He slipped his arm through Amber's, and they walked off.

"Yeah, tell your mom," Roland said, staying behind a moment. He shook his fist. "Cake." He lumbered off after Stevie.

"Wouldn't it be great to smell like cake?" Lee sighed from the far end of the table.

"Yes, it would," Marvin said, his nostrils burning from his own shower-kraut smell. "Yes, it would."

3

The Screaming Pink Raisin

Marvin walked in the front door of his house and plunked his backpack on the floor. "I'm home," he called out, without much enthusiasm.

Marvin's mom looked in from the kitchen. "Not so loud," she said in an exaggerated whisper, and pointed up at the ceiling. "Baby Harry is sleeping." She was about to go back into the kitchen, when she did a double take and stopped. "Why on earth are you wearing your gym shirt?" she said.

Marvin looked down at the T-shirt, which he had changed into after lunch, when he couldn't take the stench of fermented cabbage any longer. His other shirt was wadded up in a soggy, smelly ball at the bottom of his bag. "Someone dumped sauerkraut on me."

"Now, who would do a thing like that?" she asked.

"It was one of Little Stevie's friends," Marvin said bitterly.

"Oh! One of Stevie's friends! Well how nice. I'm sure he didn't mean to," she said, smiling. "I'm so glad that you and your cousin are finally in the same school together."

"But he *did* do it on purpose—" Marvin said loudly, before being cut off by a high-pitched wail from upstairs.

His mother scowled. "Now look what you've done. Honestly, Marvin." She brushed past him and hurried upstairs to calm Baby Harry.

Having a baby brother hadn't sounded so bad to Marvin when his dad first told him about it all those months ago.

"Marvin," his dad had asked, "how would you like a new friend?"

Marvin had thought about this. "Is it going to cost us money?" he'd asked.

"Well, yeah, but—that's not the point. This friend is going to be related to you."

"Cousin Stevie's not coming over, is he?" Marvin had asked with some trepidation.

"No," his dad had said, and sighed. "You're going to have a baby brother!"

"A baby brother?"

"Yes," his dad said, "so you'll always have a friend you can count on. You know, like Wilbur and Orville Wright. Or . . . the Ringling Brothers. Or Cain and Abel."

But when he finally arrived a few weeks ago, little Harrison Watson Jr. didn't measure up to Marvin's expectations of a friend. Marvin tried to show him his collection of comic books, but Baby Harry just threw up on them. He tried to take him outside to show him the crab apple tree—which produced the finest crab apples in the county—but Baby Harry just screamed until Marvin's mom ordered them back inside.

In fact, mostly what he did was scream, all day and all night, like he was doing now. Scream, holler, yell, whine—and poop. He was pink and wrinkled and screamed. Marvin was short on pals at the moment, but he still wasn't sure that he wanted to be friends with a screaming pink raisin.

Marvin trudged up the stairs to his room. Their house was small, a two-bedroom row home in Butcherville's Crown Roast neighborhood. The area had been a thriving blue-collar district when it was built during the 1940s, but now the homes here were merely old. Upstairs, Marvin's room faced his parents' room across the hallway. A shared bathroom was at the end of the hall, right next to the door to the attic stairs.

It was a perfectly good house, which Marvin's grandfather had bought on the salary of a door-to-door Pork Loaf salesman. When he retired to Florida, he had given the house to Marvin's dad, and they had all lived there ever since. Unlike Little Stevie, Marvin's family hadn't inherited piles of money. His mom had never asked for any of the Upton family wealth, and Marvin's family had made do on his dad's modest salary as a research scientist. They were hardly poor, despite Stevie's insistence that they were, but they also weren't filthy rich.

Marvin closed his bedroom door behind him to shut out the sounds of his mother cooing to Baby Harry. On the back of the door was tacked a large poster of his favorite comic-book character, Fearless Phil: The Man Who Laughs in the Face of Fear. On a day like today, Marvin wished he could be more like Phil and just laugh off the fear and humiliation.

Marvin peeled off his undersize gym shirt and changed into a clean T-shirt. He removed the stinky shower-kraut shirt from his backpack and threw it into the hamper. He also pulled out his algebra textbook, which was a little cabbage-y from contact with his shirt. Marvin knew he should get started on his homework, but, as he went over to clear off his desk, he saw his chemistry set laid out across it and threw the textbook back into his bag. He'd had just about enough of middle school for one day.

Instead, he decided to immerse himself in his latest project: attempting to mix up a new flavor of Pork Loaf International Fruit Flavored Punch, also known as "Pork Punch." Mr. Piggly Winks, the dapper pig mascot of PLI, smiled knowingly at Marvin from the label of the drink mix package on his desk.

Marvin had always enjoyed tinkering and experimenting, and his dad's job gave him access to more things than came with the average kid's chemistry set. Marvin's dad, Harrison Watson Sr., was a research scientist at Pork Loaf International, in charge of making the Pork Loaf Log Roll more nutritious, and he brought home real ingredients from the PLI lab for Marvin to experiment with.

Although PLI had made its fortune selling processed, enriched meats, it had long since branched out into beverages, fruit snacks, cosmetics, and household cleaning products. Pork Punch was the go-to beverage, found in school vending machines and at every picnic and family function—which was why Marvin wished someone over there would try to make it taste a little bit better.

Marvin unscrewed the lab jars that contained the various ingredients: food dyes, fruit-flavoring agents, nutrient mixes, stabilizers, destabilizers, aroma enhancers, and so on. He began by measuring out the standard flavor components and sweeteners into a large Erlenmeyer flask. He wasn't careful with his proportions. Although Marvin liked science, he couldn't approach it with the same rigor as his father. His methods were more . . . improvisational. They tended to yield surprising results. Why, the things he had learned about Pork Loaf by running high voltages through it could fill a library. There was the Pork Loaf variation on the classic potato-powered-clock experiment, but

Marvin found that boring—there wasn't enough wow factor in a digital clock quietly running off a hunk of luncheon meat. Much more intriguing was his discovery that the Pork Loaf Log Roll would glow like a night-light when plugged into 120-volt alternating current. Of course, when he attempted to wire in a Big 'Un—the steak-size version of Pork Loaf—he blew out the power grid in a ten-block radius. Some would see that as a setback, but Marvin felt that no great scientific breakthrough was ever achieved without risk.

He was just beginning to add a few drops of the potent pink food dye that gave the punch its characteristically pork-like color, when Baby Harry suddenly shrieked. Marvin's head jerked in the direction of the scream, and his hand jerked, too. Before he realized it, he had inadvertently poured the entire container of dye into the flask. The flask's contents bubbled and churned, turning a grotesque green for a moment before returning to a slightly less distressing bright pink. He lifted the glass to his lips and took a huge gulp—which he promptly spat right back into the container. The flavor was . . . awful. Surprisingly awful.

"Ugh," he said, spitting over and over again to try

to get the taste out of his mouth. "That's the worst batch yet. Maybe it'll improve after it ages a while." He poured it into four test tubes set in a metal rack.

Marvin heard a door slam downstairs and guessed that his dad was home from work. Sure enough, Harry Watson Sr. came up the stairs, briefly talked with Marvin's mom, and then knocked on Marvin's door before poking his head inside.

"In the middle of a critical experiment, Dr. Watson?" Marvin's dad asked.

"You could say that," Marvin said. "I'm trying to create a better-tasting Pork Punch." He cast a suspicious eye at the test tubes. "But I don't think I'm there yet."

"Ah," said Marvin's dad. "That's my little lab assistant." He tousled Marvin's hair.

"Dad!" Marvin said, batting away his hand in irritation but smiling. "I'm not *that* little anymore."

"No, of course not!" his dad said. "Looks like you've got a real lab of your own right here."

When Marvin was younger, his father had often taken him to work, dressed him up in an oversize lab coat, and let him pretend to help with experiments.

His dad had always encouraged him and spent time with him—but he hadn't been around as much since Baby Harry came along.

"Can you take a break for dinner?" his dad asked.

"What are we having?" Marvin said.

"Your favorite—spaghetti and meatballs."

"With real meat? Not Pork Loaf?" Marvin asked, his eyes wide.

"Sure," his dad said, smiling. "After all, I bet you've had a busy day. There's nothing like the first day of middle school."

"I hope not," Marvin said, then followed his dad downstairs.

When he walked into the kitchen, Marvin saw that it was true—his mom had made a glorious feast. As he sat down, she laid a plate heaped with a great mound of spaghetti and sauce in front of him. She scooped up the two biggest meatballs from the serving bowl. Each was the size of his fist. She plunked them on top of the mountain of spaghetti. Then came Marvin's favorite part. He picked up the rotary cheese grater—they had real Parmesan cheese tonight, not that stuff in the green can—and cranked the handle to let fall a dusting of Parmesan "snow" on the "mountaintop." He knew it seemed a little childish, but he still loved it.

As Marvin stuffed a forkful of spaghetti and meatball into his mouth, his dad cleared his throat.

"Marvin," he said, "you're a young man now, aren't you?"

"Myef," he said around a mouthful of food. "I gueff fo."

"And young men can be on their own," his dad continued. "They can be farther away from their parents. But your baby brother is very little. He needs to be closer to his parents."

"He's already in your room," Marvin said, chewing.

"Not *that* close," his mom said, looking tired.

"Anyway," his dad continued, "we need to set up your bedroom as a nursery for the baby so your mom and I can get some sleep. So you're going to have to move up to the attic."

Marvin choked on his spaghetti and meatballs. He began coughing loudly.

"The attic?" he asked, his eyes watering from the

hunk of meatball stuck in his windpipe. "But it's not even finished."

"It's the only practical thing to do," his dad said. "And besides, you need a quiet place where you can study. Middle school is going to be a lot tougher than elementary school. But I know you'll do well."

A second later, Marvin let loose a hacking cough that shook the whole table. As the glob of meat and pasta finally worked its way free of his throat, he noticed— too late—his remaining meatball tumbling off his plate to land with a splat on the floor. He stared sadly at his lost meatball with watery eyes.

"Oh, don't cry, sweetie," his mom said, leaning across the table and pinching his cheek, a dreamy expression on her face. "Just think—now my little angel will be even closer to heaven."

Marvin didn't know what to think about that.

After dinner, Marvin and his dad took apart Marvin's bed and carried it and the rest of his stuff up the steep staircase to the attic.

"Boy, I used to love playing up here when I was a little kid," Marvin's dad said as he threw open the door and turned on the light. "There's a great set of encyclopedias," he said, pointing to a pile of dusty boxes. "And my old ham radio and telescope," he added, pointing to another pile of boxes. "And the games!" He pointed to yet another pile of dusty boxes.

Marvin said nothing. He opened up an old wardrobe to hang his clothes, but it was already full of musty coats. He pulled out a long wool overcoat and saw that it was riddled with small holes.

"What are these holes from?" Marvin asked.

His dad glanced over from where he was assembling the bed. "Oh, that's your grandfather's old coat from World War II. He must have left it up here when he moved to Florida." He took the coat from Marvin's hands and gave it a good shake, sending a trio of moths fluttering off. "See—moths made the holes. Moth larvae like to eat wool." He tossed the coat on a box and went back downstairs to get more stuff.

Marvin sat glumly on a cardboard box, which began to sag. He looked around at all his things—his bed, his dresser, his clothes. Nothing looked at home up here.

His dad came back up the stairs, holding Marvin's chemistry set. "Here we go," he said. "We need to find a special place for this."

"Put it in the corner," Marvin said glumly. "In the dark."

"How about right here at your bedside," Marvin's dad said, ignoring him. "There!"

From downstairs, they could hear the all-too-familiar wail of Baby Harry starting up again.

"Honey," Marvin's mom called. "Can you come down here and help me?"

"Be right there," Marvin's dad shouted down. He walked to the door, then stopped and looked over at Marvin. "Now, don't stay up too late working on your science experiment," he said brightly.

"Don't worry," Marvin said. "I won't."

After his father shut the door, Marvin glanced once more around his new home. He knew the row houses in downtown Butcherville had been built during the postwar boom of the late 1940s, when the aroma of sizzling meat products filled every home and it was said that the very streets were paved with pork. Housing had been in great demand then, and builders found that row homes could be built quickly and affordably. In retrospect, they could have done a slightly better job. For instance, Marvin realized that he could see into his neighbor's attic through a hole in the wall, and he dimly glimpsed the next attic beyond that, too. He guessed that, in the postwar unity, no one really cared that their attics ran together.

The attic reminded Marvin of something out of a monster movie. It was dark and cold and spooky, and even the cobwebs were covered with dust. The old floorboards were uneven and creaked every time he took a step. There were mouse holes in the corners— the corners that he could even see into—and he thought he spotted a huge spider scuttling along the bare rafters.

With no prospects for a better evening ahead, Marvin decided to call it a day. A miserable, terrible day—that apparently wasn't done with him yet. As he started getting ready for bed, he noticed that one of the attic windows had warped and wouldn't completely close. A draft gusted through. Even though it was only September, the air held a chill of autumn.

Shivering—both from cold and fear—Marvin put on his heaviest flannel pajamas, pulled the chain to turn off the bare overhead lightbulb, and crawled into bed. Lying there, with his hair pressed against the pillow, the almost-forgotten scent of vinegar from the shower-kraut suddenly invaded his nose. He jerked upright in bed, banging his head sharply against a low-hanging rafter.

"Gah!" Marvin shouted, clutching the swiftly rising bump on his head. Dust rained down on him from above, triggering a trio of violent sneezes.

Almost on cue, Baby Harry began to wail.

"Marvin!" his mom shouted from downstairs. "Will you keep it down up there?"

"Sorry, Mom," he said, rubbing his head. He sighed and lay back down on his dusty, vinegar-scented pillow. Marvin sincerely hoped that this was the worst day of his life, because he didn't think he could survive another one like it. Or if it wasn't, he at least hoped the roof would cave in on him.

With that thought in mind, Marvin drifted off to a nightmare-filled sleep.

Interlude

The cat chased the mouse through the moonlit yard. He was a confident predator. This was his territory. He knew every piece of the landscape, every bush, every rock, every garbage can. The mouse wouldn't last long.

He watched the mouse take a left turn into the alley alongside the row houses. The cat knew it was a dead end, so he slowed his pursuit. The mouse couldn't escape now.

But as the cat entered the shadowy alleyway, something seemed different. Was it a new scent? A strange shape? An odd sound?

There it was: a crunching noise. And the smell of blood.

The cat halted his advance. Something had gotten to his prey first. He couldn't let that go. This was his territory, and he had to defend it. He stalked deeper into the shadows, claws and teeth at the ready.

"Ahhh," called a strange voice from the darkness ahead. "So, *thou wilt be as valiant as the wrathful dove, or most magnanimous mouse.*"

The cat hesitated again. The voice sounded human . . . but the scent was all wrong. The cat started to back away, his ears flat against his head.

"*The cat will mew, and dog will have his day,*" the voice called out. "In other words, you're next, you illiterate feline!"

The cat hissed and shrieked as a large shape jumped out of the shadows.

Then the alleyway was silent.

4

The Evil Robot Girl

Marvin didn't sleep very well his first night in the attic. When he woke in the morning, he half remembered a strange dream in which a giant moth was sitting on his bed, chewing on his bedspread. It then picked up a book from one of the old, dusty boxes in the attic before it walked into the shadows, whistling. Marvin wondered if the shower-kraut had seeped through his scalp and into his brain. Although, when he examined his bedspread, it *did* seem to be worn thin in a few places. He couldn't remember if it had been like that before he moved up to the attic or not. And that bothered him.

In addition to strange dreams and not having a good night's sleep, Marvin was worried that people might see his underwear again. So he picked out a nice pair, just in case. The pressures of middle school were many and varied.

Marvin made it through first period—health class—without major incident, although the discussions of human anatomy led to inevitable catcalls asking Marvin to model in his underwear. His second-period algebra class passed without embarrassment, but Marvin could feel himself falling further behind as he failed to grasp the difficult concepts.

He walked into his third-period science class and scanned the room. Most of the students who had already arrived were crowded into the back rows of desks. Marvin soon saw why: Lee Skluzacek was sitting near the front of the room.

By sheer reflex, and perhaps some olfactory instinct of self-preservation buried deep within his genes, Marvin began to walk toward the back of the room. But then he paused, thinking about how Lee had, thus far, been almost the only person in the whole school to treat him like a human being rather than as an object of ridicule. He turned and, against his nose's better judgment, walked around and sat in the front row, just ahead of Lee.

"Hey, Marvin," Lee said. It was a chilly day, and Lee's odor had been tamped down by the layers of shirts and sweatshirts he was wearing. "Want a mint?" he said, holding out a plastic box. "I love these things."

Marvin took one and crunched into it. "Your breath *is* surprisingly minty fresh," he told Lee. "Thanks." He wondered, for the first time, what it was, exactly, that caused Lee's odor. He had always presumed it had something to do with poor hygiene, but that didn't seem to be the case. Now he could see that Lee's hands and fingernails were immaculate. His hair was neatly trimmed into a short brush atop his head. And his clothes were cleaner than Marvin's, quite frankly. Marvin supposed it was just one of those eternal mysteries that would never be solved.

Just then, as he swallowed the last bit of mint, he heard something. Or rather, a lot of somethings. From out in the hallway, a strange collection of noises approached. Mechanical clankings, creakings, and beepings.

"What's that noise?" asked Lee.

"It sounds like a robot," Marvin offered. "An evil robot." Although that seemed unlikely, the past day or two had taught him to expect the worst. He could just picture some evil robot escaped from a mad scientist's lair, rampaging and destroying and administering wedgies to unwary sixth graders. Marvin nervously fiddled with the elastic waistband of his underwear.

Just then, in answer to his nightmares, a tall figure appeared in the doorway, covered in metal and sinister red lights. Marvin gasped, and Lee buried his face in his book, whimpering. As the class bell rang, a terrifying chorus of beeps and buzzes erupted from the robot's body. Was it angered? Was it going to attack? Gradually, the buzzing and chirping subsided, and, as the figure emerged from the doorway, Marvin could see that it was just a girl. Granted, a girl with a lot of gear.

"This better be science class," she said. "I'm always very punctual."

The girl sat down next to Lee and Marvin with a rattle and a clank. She seemed to be wrapped in metal and electronics from head to toe. Her left leg was strapped into a large knee brace. Half a dozen gadgets, from fitness trackers to graphing calculators to mobile phones, hung from her waist. And on her head, in addition to thick-lensed glasses, was an enormous contraption of steel and wires the likes of which Marvin had never seen before.

Behind Marvin, Lee peered up from his textbook. "Who are you?" he asked.

"I'm Fatima," the girl said. "Fatima Curie."

"Are you from the future?" Lee asked in an awe-struck voice.

"What?" the girl said. "No, I transferred here from Swineheart Academy."

"I think what he means is, what's with . . . ?" Marvin gestured vaguely at her face.

"I'll have you know that this is special orthodontic headgear," Fatima said. "It's going to straighten my teeth so I'll be superbeautiful *and* supersmart, so I'll never have to talk to Neanderthals like you again!" She glared first at Marvin and then at Lee.

"Please don't kill me, robot," Lee whispered.

"You should learn to accept people's differences, you smelly pig," she said. Lee sank lower in his chair.

"And *you*," she said, whirling at Marvin. "You should be the last person to make fun of someone for their appearance. At least *I'm* not parading around in my undergarments."

"You heard about that?" Marvin said. "That's never going away, is it?"

At that exact moment, Stevie Upton walked into the room and said, "Hey, Tarzan! Looks like you found yourself a Jane!" He sniffed the air with displeasure. "And it smells like you found a monkey to be your sidekick, too."

"Oh, Stevie," said Fatima. "Coming to infect the public-school system with your low-grade brain function and kindergarten humor?"

"You know it, brace-face," Stevie said with a wink. "So glad you followed me here from Swineheart. Your scowl always brightens my day." He took a seat across the room, as far away from Lee as possible.

"I can't believe we're related," said Marvin.

"You and Stevie Upton?" said Fatima. "I'm not surprised. I can see the family resemblance. You're both inconsiderate morons."

"So, the two of you went to Swineheart together?" Marvin said.

"Yes, and I'd still be in private school if this Podunk company town had a private middle school," she said.

Across the room, Stevie perked up. "Podunk company town? Hey, now—don't talk that way about our town *or* the company. PLI is the lifeblood of our fair city. Why, both my father and Tarzan's work for PLI."

"I would never trust anyone who works for Pork Loaf," Fatima said. "They're up to no good in those labs."

"What do you mean?" Marvin asked, indignant. "They've added eighty-seven essential nutrients to their mix since my dad started working there."

"That's exactly what I'm saying," said Fatima, her voice dropping low. "Who knows if the human body can even *take* that much nutrition?"

The science teacher, Miss Sweeney, hurried into the room. "Sorry I'm late, class, but the supply company sent us live frogs instead of dead ones for dissection, and some of them got away before I could pack them up for return." Outside, a janitor ran down the hall after a furiously leaping frog.

"Let's start off by talking about the scientific method," Miss Sweeney said. She picked up a piece of chalk and began to write the steps of the scientific method on the chalkboard. Marvin opened his notebook to copy down the information, but Fatima kept talking to him under her breath.

"Step one," said Miss Sweeney. "Define the question."

"Have you noticed that all the stray cats in this town seem to be vanishing?" asked Fatima.

"What?" said Marvin.

"Step two," said Miss Sweeney. "Gather information and resources."

"It's all right here in the *National Examiner*," Fatima said, pulling a tablet from her bag. She woke up the device and scrolled past stories with headlines like "Ratboy: Dating Tips from Half-Rat, Half-Man Hunk," "Aliens Put Whoopee Cushions on All the Seats of Canadian Parliament: Chamber Sounds in Accord for First Time in Years," and "Seattle Man Fulfills Prophecy by Growing Second Head out of Elbow." She clicked through to a story whose headline read, "Cat-Tastrophe! Dozens of Cats Disappear in Sleepy Small Town."

"So what?" said Marvin.

"Step three," said Miss Sweeney. "Form hypothesis."

"Isn't it obvious?" Fatima hissed. "Pork Loaf's been getting so much flak from animal rights activists that they've gone underground. They're stealing those cats, putting them in cages, and secretly testing cosmetics on them."

"Step four," said Miss Sweeney. "Perform experiment and collect data."

"Is that why that cage is on your face?" Marvin asked Fatima. "Were you one of their experiments gone wrong?"

"I'm astonished at your rudeness," said Fatima. "And at your lack of concern over this important issue."

"Step five," said Miss Sweeney. "Analyze data."

"But there's no proof of any kind," said Marvin.

"Oh yeah? This morning my neighbor Mrs. Fishman told me that there used to be twenty cats living in the alleyway behind her house, and today there were only two," said Fatima. "That's a ninety percent drop in alley cat population."

"Step six," said Miss Sweeney. "Interpret data and draw conclusions that serve as a starting point for new hypotheses."

"You're crazy," said Marvin.

"And finally, step seven," said Miss Sweeney. "Publish results."

Marvin turned back to his notes, scurrying to copy down everything Miss Sweeney had gone over. He had fallen behind listening to Fatima's nonsense. At the bottom of the page, he scribbled one last important reminder: *Fatima is a nutjob*. When he finally looked up, he saw that everyone else in the class was gathering into small clusters. On the chalkboard was written: *Choose your groups.*

"What's going on?" he asked.

"We're choosing lab partners," said Fatima.

Marvin looked around the room. Everybody else had formed tight groups of three or four people. He looked at Lee, who had not joined a group yet. Then he looked at Fatima, who was in the same boat. They were the only three unattached people.

"Put 'er there, partner," said Lee, holding his hand out to Marvin. "I mean, partners," he added, putting his other hand out toward Fatima. Neither Marvin nor Fatima made any move to shake Lee's hand.

"Great," said Marvin, wearily rubbing his forehead.

"That's just what *I* thought!" said Lee. "I'm sure we're going to get along just great."

"Sure," said Fatima. She looked over at the notebook page where Marvin had written *Fatima is a nutjob* and said coldly to Lee, "*He* can take notes."

Interlude

The farmer had pulled up the ramp to the chicken coop for the night, so that no foxes could climb in and eat his prize poultry. Little did he know that by this time no foxes remained within the city limits—and that the real danger came not from below, but from above.

A dark shape moved with unnatural grace across the ceiling of the henhouse. Below it, two dozen chickens slept peaceful chicken-sleep on their roosts, dreaming of cracked corn.

"Stalk on, stalk on," said the shape. *"The fowl sits."*

One of the chickens opened an eye and peered around the darkened coop. There was nothing there. It was only her imagination.

Just before she settled back down to sleep, she felt a sharp sensation in her wing and let out a panicked squawk, sending loose feathers flying.

"For a fish without a fin, there's a fowl without a feather: If a crow help us in, sirrah, we'll pluck a crow together."

In response, the chicken let out a confused *ba-gawk?*

"Oh, never mind," said the predator, snatching its victim away.

5

The Algebra Lesson

Marvin sat in his attic room, trying desperately to understand the foreign language that was algebra. He had stared at the squiggles on the page of his textbook for so long that they were beginning to dance and swim before his eyes. To add to his frustration, Baby Harry was practicing yodeling downstairs. Marvin was astounded by his brother's ability to discover and execute increasingly irritating forms of expression. He admired the effort, but the noise was making it impossible for him to concentrate. At last, he could stand it no more.

Marvin looked for something to plug his ears. He tried cotton balls, but they helped only a little. He thought maybe mashed potatoes would do the trick, but there had been no leftovers from dinner. He was afraid his sculpting clay would harden permanently if he stuck it in his ears.

Not a room in the house was safe from the wailing of Baby Harry. As Marvin desperately searched the attic for some solution, his eye fell upon the hole in the wall—the one that led into the neighboring attics. He wondered if it was quiet enough next door to study.

Marvin grabbed his flashlight and his algebra book. He clicked on the flashlight and examined the hole. At some point, someone had snapped off the frail wooden slats to make a sizable opening—one that was large enough for him to crawl through. Marvin took a breath, and in he went.

On the other side, things looked much the same. The neighbors' attic was the same size and shape as Marvin's, and just as full of clutter.

As he prepared to find a spot to settle down and study in, Marvin noticed a flickering blue glow coming from the far side of the attic. He made his way through the boxes and old suitcases, past dusty dolls and deflated footballs, toward the source of the light. In the far wall, there was another hole, and through it, he could see light and hear noises. It sounded like a television. Had some other poor kid been moved up to the attic? Was *his* baby brother equally loud? Marvin's heart swelled with thoughts of camaraderie—perhaps they could form a brotherhood. A fraternity of the attic children. With that thought in mind, Marvin plunged through the hole to meet his new friend.

Marvin was surprised to find not one, but three attic dwellers beyond the wall. He was even more surprised to find that they were not children. The flickering blue light of the television danced off their long antennae and large, multifaceted eyes. Their bloated, furry bodies and long wings were stuffed awkwardly into lumpy armchairs. And their many limbs waved wildly in response to the action on the television. They were giant moths, and Marvin saw that they were watching baseball.

A tall, skinny moth said, "By my calculations, he is now up to ninety-eight pitches. His coach will surely take him out soon."

"You're nuts, Aristotle," said a short, round moth, who was only a little bit taller than Marvin. "He's got perfect control over that fastball. Oh, and those graphics at the bottom of the screen TELL US how many pitches he's thrown, you uptight stick-bug."

Marvin reflected that, not only were these giant moths watching baseball, but they could talk—and they had an excellent grasp of the fundamentals.

The largest of the three, over seven feet tall and nearly as wide, finally turned its attention to Marvin. It looked him up and down with its inhuman compound eyes and asked him, "Did you bring anything to eat?"

"I—I don't know," said Marvin. He held up his algebra textbook. "All I brought was this book. Can you eat that?"

"If we could eat books, we would be stuffed by now," said the skinny moth, who was apparently named Aristotle. He waved a leg at a pile of dusty books behind him. Marvin thought he saw some of his dad's old encyclopedias among them.

"You know," said the short, round moth, "when you go over to someone's house to watch a game, you're supposed to bring snacks."

"Abraham's got a point," said the largest moth. "And that sweater looks tasty." He made a smacking sound with his mandibles. Marvin was worried about losing the sweater—his mom had given it to him for Christmas—but he was more worried about keeping three giant, hungry insects happy. He quickly removed the sweater and handed it to the moths, who tore it into three pieces and began munching.

For a long moment, there was nothing but the sounds of slurping and chewing and baseball. Finally, the short, round moth glanced over at Marvin and said, "Not much of a conversationalist, are you?"

"Are you planning to eat me next?" Marvin asked nervously.

"If we could eat you, we would have already gobbled you up in your sleep," said Aristotle.

"Oh," said Marvin. "That's reassuring."

"Don't think Ahab here didn't try," said the short one, Abraham, pointing to the largest moth.

"He's just kidding," said Ahab.

"Yeah—hah," said Marvin. "That's a good one." He studied the giant moths for a moment. "So, where did you guys come from?"

"What do you mean?" said Abraham. "We live here. You're the one who came over."

"What I mean is, why are you so big?" asked Marvin.

"I don't know," said Abraham. "Why are you so small?"

"What?" Marvin said in disbelief. "No. You're a *giant moth*."

"And you're a giant pain in my butt!" said Abraham.

"But moths aren't supposed to talk," insisted Marvin, bewildered.

"Is this one of those only-speak-when-you're-spoken-to things?" Abraham said angrily. "Don't oppress me, man!"

"Sorry," Marvin apologized. He dropped his eyes and noticed his chemistry set was sitting on the coffee table in front of the moths. All four test tubes were empty. "Hey! My science experiment!"

"It was yummy," said the giant, Ahab. "You got any more?"

"You drank my experiment?" Marvin asked.

"Yeah, we each had a test tube of it," said Abraham.

"What about the fourth one?"

"How should I know? What am I, your accountant?" said Abraham. "Keep track of your own stuff."

"Whatcha reading?" Ahab asked Marvin, slurping up the last string of Marvin's sweater like a strand of spaghetti.

Marvin looked down at the textbook in his hands. "Algebra," he said.

"Algebra is child's play," said Aristotle, waving a leg dismissively. "You should try calculus."

"Well, I don't even understand this first page," Marvin said.

"Bring it here," said Aristotle. "Let me look at that."

"How do you know algebra?" Marvin asked.

"We've been reading encyclopedias for days," said Aristotle. "There's not much else to do up here between ball games."

An hour later, Marvin understood the first chapter quite well, although he had never had a tutor with so many arms. He thanked the moths and crawled, sweaterless, back to his own attic. He was wiser, but colder, for the experience.

Interlude

Of all the pigs in the yard, James was the most beautiful. He knew it, the farmer knew it, and soon, the entire town of Butcherville would know it, too. At 240 pounds of pink pigness, James was a shoo-in to win the blue ribbon at the upcoming Seventy-Fifth Annual Pork Loaf Harvest Festival. He had even developed a little strut as he walked by the other hogs in the yard. They didn't like it, but they knew, on this farm, James was king.

As dusk settled upon Butcherville, James made one final circuit of his kingdom before bedding down in fine golden straw, satisfied that everything was right with the world.

From a dark corner of the sty came a cold voice. *"O monstrous beast! How like a swine he lies! Grim death, how foul and loathsome is thine image!"*

James, who hadn't heard the voice, snorted comfortably, oblivious as the dark shape descended. It sank its dripping fangs into James's rump, causing the pig to let out a snort and a squeal—but it was too late. His hindquarters were paralyzed. James's 240 prize-winning-pounds weighed him down as he clawed at the earth with his front hooves, trying vainly to drag himself away.

The other pigs, awakened by the commotion, shrugged and went back to bed. They were all going to be someone's dinner eventually—but at least now, one of them had a shot at that blue ribbon.

6

The Meeting in the Dark

The next morning, Marvin had a pop quiz in algebra class. To his utter surprise, he made it through with a B. Apparently his insect tutors—creepy as they were—had done a pretty good job.

That evening at dinner, Marvin's father asked, "How was school?"

Marvin replied, "Not too bad. I got a B on my algebra quiz."

"Good," his father said. "I thought you said you were having trouble in that class. Did you get some help?"

"Yeah. I found some giant moths living in the attic. They know algebra, and they said they'll teach me calculus, too, in a couple of years."

"Hardy-har-har," his father said. "Wise guy."

"Eat your Pork Loaf, honey," his mother said.

Marvin realized that there were some things about his life that his parents just couldn't understand.

At school, Fatima had spent their science class sitting in stony silence, pretending that Marvin didn't exist. He hadn't known how to reach out to her to smooth things over, and he hadn't been entirely sure he had a reason to bother. But the experience with the moths was so strange that he felt he had to share it with someone, and the weirdness of it seemed right up her alley. When Marvin passed her in the halls the following Monday, he gave her a tentative wave. Fatima shot him a dirty look and clanked off to her next class.

In science class that Wednesday, Miss Sweeney told them once again to get into their groups. Marvin, Lee, and Fatima sat at their lab table, not talking as usual. After several minutes had passed, Fatima finally turned to Marvin and said, "Am I a *walnut* or a *peanut* or a *cashew*?"

"A what?" Marvin replied, confused.

"You wrote that I was a nut. What kind of nut am I?"

"Actually, I wrote that you were a nut*job*," Marvin said, pulling out his notebook. "See?"

"Wow. You take excellent notes," Lee said. "Can I copy those?" He took Marvin's notebook and began scribbling furiously.

"Oh. Well I wouldn't expect you to understand the truth about the weird things that happen in this town," said Fatima. "Your whole family is in league with Pork Loaf."

"Actually, I know a little about some weird things," Marvin said. He paused. "What if I told you a secret about something really strange?"

Fatima's jaw dropped—as much as it could drop, being held in place by her orthodontic headgear.

"A secret? What is it?" she asked breathlessly. "Is it about the fifteen cases of mummified ankle bones? Or the disappearing cats? Or the subliminal brainwashing signal transmitted with Pork Loaf commercials?"

"No," Marvin said. "It's this: There are moths in my attic."

"That's your secret?" Fatima said. "How is that

a secret? Here's a news flash—there are rocks in your head."

"Will you let me finish?" Marvin replied. "They're giant, superintelligent moths."

"Uh-huh," said Fatima. "Sure they are. Compared with you, maybe."

"No, I'm serious," Marvin insisted. "They can speak, and they helped me with my algebra." He showed her his pop quiz, with a *B* emblazoned in red marker at the top.

"You're right," Fatima said. "I don't believe you're smart enough to do that on your own. But how do I know you're not just pulling my leg?"

Marvin sat openmouthed for several seconds, trying to come up with an answer that didn't involve a knee-brace joke.

"Attention, class," Miss Sweeney said. "Your group project will be to use the scientific method to conduct an experiment. The subject of the experiment is your choice. Just be sure to document your procedures and results, and be prepared to present your findings in front of the class in two weeks."

Marvin turned to Fatima. "Look. We have to get together to figure out this homework assignment, anyway. Why don't we meet at my house on Saturday, and I'll introduce you to the moths."

Fatima warily agreed.

"Nutjob!" Lee exclaimed, scribbling down the last of Marvin's notes. "Got it!" He put down his pencil. "Thanks, Marvin," he said, and returned the notebook.

Early Saturday afternoon, Harry Watson Sr. was taking paper plates and cups from the pantry for Baby Harry's barbecue when the doorbell rang. As he opened the door he caught a whiff of a foul odor.

"Are you here to see Marvin?" he asked the boy and girl standing on the stoop. They nodded. "You'd better get inside," he said. "I think the sewers are backing up again."

"I'm sorry, sir, I think that's me," said Lee as they stepped inside. He handed Marvin's dad a preprinted calling card. "My grandmother makes me carry these."

The card read: *My name is Lee Skluzacek. I apologize for the smell. I do bathe regularly. My doctors do not know the cause of my condition. Thank you for your consideration.*

In the next room, startled by the stench, Baby Harry began to wail.

"Um. Marvin's up in his room, in the attic. Why don't you do your schoolwork there," Marvin's dad tactfully suggested.

They began climbing the stairs.

"And close the door," Marvin's dad called up after them.

Marvin was sitting on his bed reading his favorite comic book, *Fearless Phil: The Man Who Laughs in the Face of Fear*. Phil was an unapologetically reckless idiot who saved people by diving headfirst into danger and never thinking about the consequences. Marvin wasn't sure why, but the character appealed to him on a deep level. He looked up as his guests entered the room.

"That was uncomfortable," Fatima announced. "I was sure your dad would ask me what I knew about Pork Loaf's involvement in the Iran-Contra Affair."

"He's not like that," said Marvin.

"Have you told him about the giant, superintelligent M-O-T-H-S?" she asked.

"Giant math?" Lee exclaimed in horror. "I thought we were working on our science project."

"Not math, moths," Fatima declared, then clapped her hand over her mouth in alarm and glanced toward the door. "Do you think he heard that?" she whispered.

"I wouldn't worry about him," Marvin said. "I tried to tell my parents about it the other night, but they just didn't get it."

"So, where *are* the you-know-whats?" Fatima asked. Just then, an inhuman, bloodcurdling wail pierced the air, followed by a shrieking voice from the space beyond the attic wall.

"Are you blind, ump?" came the scream. "He was safe. Safe!"

Fatima and Lee jumped at the sound, and hugged each other in fear. "What was that?" Fatima whispered.

Meanwhile, Marvin was already clambering into the hole in the wall. "Come on," he said. "They're just watching baseball."

Fatima suddenly realized she was clutching Lee and released him. Then she composed her face into a tough frown and followed Marvin into the hole.

As they made their way through the cluttered passageway of the adjacent attic, Fatima asked Marvin, "What are the moths like?"

"They're stranger than you can imagine," Marvin said.

"Are they dangerous?" she asked.

"I don't think so," said Marvin. "Just very sarcastic."

As before, an eerie, bluish phantom light flickered through the final hole in the wall, accompanied by the sounds of baseball, a sports announcer's nasal voice, and burps and mutterings. The kids stood in front of the glowing opening, which looked to be some portal to another world.

"Well, we're here," Marvin said, crouching down in front of the hole. "You ready for this?"

Fatima, for once, appeared too nervous to come up with a witty reply. "Lead the way," she said.

As Marvin emerged from the far side of the hole, he saw the three moths were out of their seats in front of the television. They hopped up and down, waving their arms in an angry frenzy of motion. Abraham lifted a large bowl of snacks above his head, as though to smash it over the TV.

"Curse you and the third-base coach who waved you in!" screamed Abraham. "Why they pay grown men huge sums of money to throw a ball around—BADLY—I'll never understand."

"Turn it off," said Aristotle, waving at the TV dejectedly. "There's nothing but anguish and heartbreak in there."

Ahab bent down and turned off the TV, plunging the attic into darkness.

Lee let out a horrified wail. "Oh, oh help me. We're all going to die."

"Shut up, no we're not," Fatima said. She paused. "Are we?"

At that, Aristotle switched on a floor lamp, which cast long, menacing shadows throughout the room. "What have we here?" he said.

"These are my friends," Marvin said, "Fatima Curie and Lee Skluzacek."

"Friends?" Lee said, hopeful. "Really?"

Marvin turned to Lee and Fatima. "Let me introduce the moths," he said, and pointed to each one in turn. "This is the short, surly one, that's the tall know-it-all, and that's the big lug."

"As elegant an introduction as that was," Aristotle said, stepping forward, "allow me to give the lady our proper names. I am Aristotle, named for the great philosopher and scientist."

"How'd you get that name?" Fatima asked.

Aristotle turned and picked up a large book from a table behind him. "I was perusing the encyclopedia—"

"What's an encyclopedia?" Lee asked.

"It's like Wikipedia, only trapped in a bunch of dead trees," Fatima said. "From back in the pre-digital dark ages when we used to cut down whole forests just to make books that would be out-of-date by the time they were printed."

"As I was SAYING," Aristotle continued, glaring at Fatima with his multifaceted eyes, "I was perusing the encyclopedia and, due to my considerable intellectual gifts, the moniker seemed most appropriate."

"And them?" she asked, indicating the other two moths.

"These are Abraham and Ahab," he said, pointing first to the shorter moth and then to the massive one.

"What about you?" she asked Abraham. "Were you named after the biblical patriarch? Or Abraham Lincoln?"

"I don't know," the moth said, shrugging. "It was just the first name I came across."

Ahab waved an appendage. "And I'm called Ahab because I'm as big as a whale," he said.

"Shouldn't you be called Moby-Dick, then?" Fatima asked.

"Well, it was our first day of learning how to read, and we only had the *A* volume," Ahab said.

"That doesn't seem like a good reason," Fatima said, frowning.

"Yes, yes, it's all very interesting," Abraham said loudly. "But why are you three interrupting our doubleheader?"

"I brought them to the house to work on our science experiment for class," Marvin said.

Fatima stepped in front of Abraham and started poking and prodding at his furry body, tugging at his long, feathery antennae, and running her fingers along his shiny wings.

"Hey, watch it, lady!" Abraham said. "Don't damage the merchandise."

"Just look at those hideous eyes," Fatima said.

"And the bloated abdomen. And all those creepy arms. You're perfect! You'll make a great science project!"

"Them?" Marvin asked.

"Of course!" said Fatima. "We can run an exhaustive battery of tests on their blood and tissue samples to see what makes them different from ordinary moths. We'll get an A for sure!"

"I'll give you an A," said Abraham, snatching the *A* volume of the encyclopedia from Aristotle's hands and flinging it at Fatima, narrowly missing her head.

"Hey, watch it!" yelled Fatima.

"Abraham," said the hulking Ahab, "this is why people never come to visit us. 'Cause you're so rude." He offered a plate to the kids. "Here—have a snack." The plate was stacked with hors d'oeuvres—small wool squares on toothpicks.

"Maybe later," said Marvin.

"Wait a minute," Fatima said. "Moth larvae eat clothing, but as mature moths, shouldn't you have a plant- or nectar-based diet?"

Abraham glared at her. "So we like comfort food! Do I tell you what to eat?"

"She's right," Marvin said to the moths. "What

you eat, why you're so big, why you're so rude—all these things would be great material for a project. That is, if you guys are willing to be our science experiment."

"You mean, do we wish to be poked and prodded by you three now, and later be kidnapped by devious scientists who will poke and prod us even more before they ultimately dissect us and put our bodies on display in some museum?" asked Aristotle. He chuckled. "Pardon us if we fail to jump at the opportunity."

"I guess I see what you mean," said Marvin. He thought for a moment. "Listen, since you guys don't want to be our science experiment, do you have any ideas of what we could do instead?"

"Why don't you try to figure out why this kid smells so bad?" Abraham said as he opened the painted-over attic window to let in some fresh air. Aristotle picked up Lee and moved him to the far side of the room.

"My goodness," said Aristotle, backing away from Lee. "Do you secrete that odor as a defense mechanism? Or is it a pheromone? Are you trying to attract a female?"

"A female what?" Abraham said. "A female garbage can?"

Fatima shifted her weight, and her metal apparatus clanked. Everyone turned to look at her. "I am NOT a female garbage can!" she said.

Abraham turned back to Lee. "Have you stepped in poop?"

"Every day?" Marvin said.

"Well, I'm just ruling out the obvious."

"Did you stick something up your nose, and now it's rotting?" asked Ahab.

"Am I really going to be our science experiment?" Lee asked. "I mean, I want to help out the team, but—"

"Well, you want to get an A, don't you?" asked Fatima.

"I guess," said Lee.

"You *guess*? Listen, just go with it."

"Do you bathe?" Aristotle asked Lee.

Lee handed the moth one of his cards.

"Maybe it's an allergy," Ahab said in his slow, deep voice. "I've read that those can result in uncomfortable symptoms."

"Yeah, I'm pretty uncomfortable right now," said Abraham.

"An allergy, huh?" said Fatima. "Pollen? Grass? Ragweed?"

Lee shrugged. "I don't know why that would make me smell."

"Yeah, and then you'd only smell part of the year," said Marvin. "And we know that's not the case. It's got to be something you're exposed to every day. Maybe something that you eat?"

"A food allergy!" said Fatima. "Good! We can test that."

"How?" asked Lee.

"You should avoid eating for the next twenty-four hours, and then, once your system is cleaned out, we'll slowly reintroduce the foods you normally eat and see which one makes you smell."

"Maybe we should make it forty-eight hours, just to be sure," suggested Marvin.

"Okay," Fatima said. "Good idea."

"Hey!" Lee said. "That sounds like an awful long time."

"You know what an awful long time is?" Abraham asked. "Spending an afternoon here with you, stinky."

"I don't know if I can go two days without eating," said Lee.

"Lee—you listen to me," said Fatima, sticking her finger in his face. "If you eat anything—ANYTHING AT ALL—we will all FAIL. And I will never forgive you. And I will never forget. I will schedule not forgiving you into my online calendar every single day for the rest of my life. *Comprende?*"

"I guess . . . if it means that much to you and Marvin . . ." Lee said.

"Fascinating," Abraham said, bored. He turned to Marvin. "Could you take the pushy one and the smelly one away, now? The second game of the doubleheader is coming up, and if these two stick around, it's going to ruin my afternoon."

"What?" Fatima said, looking up. "But I'm not done yet. I have so many questions. Where did you come from? Why are you so intelligent? How can you talk?"

"Oh, we're done talking, kid," Abraham replied, hustling them through the hole in the wall. "Come back when there isn't a game on. Or better yet, never!"

Back in Marvin's room, Fatima said, "That was bracing! And we managed to figure out our class project. Well, Marvin, you aren't as useless as I thought!"

"Uh, thanks," said Marvin. The smell of charcoal smoke and sweet barbecued ribs wafted through his open window.

Lee breathed in deeply. "Wow, that smells good."

"You're both welcome to stay for the barbecue," said Marvin. He looked at Lee. "Although, *you're* not allowed to eat anything for forty-eight hours."

"Starting now," said Fatima, and she pressed a button on one of her many devices.

"You mean you *want* me to stay?" Lee said.

Marvin thought about it. He remembered that he had introduced Lee and Fatima to the moths as his friends. Were they? Did he *have* any friends anymore? Since starting middle school, since tearing his shorts in gym class, he seemed to have lost all the people he'd thought of as friends in elementary school. No one would associate with him now—except for Lee and Fatima. Lee, though smelly, was generous and kindhearted. And Fatima was smart. She wasn't just good at her classes; she also had a sharp wit (and a sharp tongue). As friends went, they might not be too bad.

Before Marvin could respond, Fatima said, "Of course he wants you to stay. We're the outliers, the outsiders. The explorers. The discoverers of giant moths! We're a team." She looked to Marvin. "Right?"

Marvin nodded. "Let's eat."

7

The Future King and Queen

When Marvin, Fatima, and Lee came downstairs, the party was already in full swing. Adults stood around in small clumps talking and eating as younger children ran through the grass squealing and giggling. People made way for Marvin and his friends, as Lee's odor, although less intense than it had been in the attic, was still off-putting for anyone trying to eat. Folding tables had been set up around the small backyard, and the edges of their paper tablecloths danced merrily in the breeze. The tables were covered with bowls of potato salad, macaroni salad, coleslaw, and chips, and heaping platters of barbecued chicken wings, pork ribs, and, of course, big slabs of grilled Pork Loaf. Marvin's dad worked the grill, wearing a faded apron that said, "PLI Pork Loaf Chili Cook-Off 2012." He cut a two-finger-thick "steak" from the extra-large version of the classic Pork Loaf Log Roll known as the "Big 'Un."

Then he threw the twelve-inch oval of meat onto the hot grill, eliciting a gout of flames from the charcoal beneath.

Lee walked up to the grill, eyes wide at the sight of all of that tasty, sizzling meat. As he watched, Marvin's dad stabbed one of the finished steaks with a barbecue fork, sending delicious juices shooting out of it. "You want one, son?" he asked Lee. "This one's ready to go—let me just sauce it up for you." Marvin's dad put the steaming steak onto a plastic plate, then brushed on some homemade barbecue sauce to finish it off. "There you go," he said, handing it to Lee.

"Mmmm," Lee murmured. Not pausing even to cut it up, he stuck the slab of meat with a fork and lifted it to his mouth, whole, to take a bite.

From across the yard, Fatima let loose a shriek, then charged, her leg brace squeaking madly as she ran straight at Lee. *We will all fail!* she screamed, then body-checked him before the steak could touch his lips. Lee crashed to the ground, and the meat spun end over end through the air, landing with a wet thud near the back fence.

Lee, still mesmerized by the sight of the meat, pulled his aching body through the grass toward his fallen steak. He crawled across the yard, Fatima clutching him by the ankles. "If you know what's good for you, you won't do it!" she said.

Just then, a large flatbed truck crashed backward through the fence, smashing it to splinters and grinding Lee's steak into the mud beneath its wheels.

"See?" said Fatima. "I told you!"

Marvin could only stare aghast at the shattered fence and torn-up shrubbery.

A burly man with cut-off sleeves and a tattoo of Mr. Piggly Winks on his shoulder descended from the cab carrying a clipboard. Harry Watson pushed his way through the startled guests and said, "What's the meaning of this?"

"Sorry about that," said the truck driver, waving his clipboard at the broken fence. "Narrow alley, and all. I've got a delivery."

Marvin's dad looked up at the cargo on the flatbed. A large boxy shape was hidden underneath a canvas shroud. "Delivery? I think you've got the wrong house."

"Are you Harry Watson Jr.?" the truck driver said, glancing at his clipboard.

"No, I'm Harry Watson Sr. Look, what—"

"Ah, I see that it's arrived," said a voice from the direction of the house.

Everyone turned to see Marvin's uncle Steve coming out of the kitchen door, accompanied by Marvin's mom. She bobbled Baby Harry in her arms, glowering at her brother and at the mess the truck had made of the yard.

"I told you, Steve, we don't need that thing," she said.

"Nonsense, Sis," Steve said with a wide smile. "Every baby needs a crib."

"Crib?" Marvin said, bewildered.

"Steve," said Marvin's dad, stepping up to shake his brother-in-law's hand. "I didn't hear you pull up, what with all the crashing and destruction. Where's your wife?"

"Oh, you know her," said Uncle Steve. "She's out in the car." He stepped over shattered fence pickets to reach the truck, where the driver was already undoing various ropes and hitches. The huge man grasped one end of the canvas shroud and whipped it off like a magician revealing a trick.

"Ta-da," the driver said in a gravelly voice.

The crib stood six feet high and ten feet wide. Its twisting rails were carved from dark mahogany and were topped with grimacing gargoyles. On the footboard was a huge golden plaque that read, UPTON. All the party guests took a step back. Baby Harry started to cry at the sight of it.

"What the heck is that?" Marvin asked.

"It's the Upton family crib, of course," said Uncle Steve, turning to look at Marvin with an oily smile. "It's been passed to the firstborn of the Upton family for seven generations. Why, Little Stevie spent a lot of time in it."

"That explains a lot about Stevie," Fatima whispered to Marvin.

"Shouldn't it *stay* in the Upton family?" Marvin said.

"This is a chance for your side of the family to make up for lost time," Uncle Steve said.

"Lost time?" Marvin said, confused. "You mean, lost time with the crib?"

"You said it, bucko," Steve said.

"It'll take up the whole nursery," said Harry.

"Yeah, and I imagine we'll have to cut out that window in order to get it inside," said Uncle Steve, sizing up the house. "Probably have to reinforce the floor to bear the weight, too. I'll have my guys come by tomorrow with a crane. You make it hard to give a gift, Harry."

Uncle Steve turned to the driver. "Cover it back up, Hal. We'll deal with it tomorrow. Today's a day to celebrate!" The driver flung the tarp back over the forbidding piece of furniture, and everyone in the yard breathed a sigh of relief. Baby Harry stopped crying.

"What smells so good?" said Uncle Steve. "Is that a Big 'Un?"

"Big 'Un," Lee sighed, gazing mournfully at the churned-up mud underneath the truck tires.

The party resumed as best it could with a large flatbed truck in the middle of it. Lee, Fatima, and Marvin went off by themselves. Fatima sat Lee down in a lawn chair in a corner of the yard—far from the food—and told him not to move. The rest of the guests seemed pleased by this arrangement, as it kept his odor at a safe distance from the merrymaking. The kids watched as the guests passed Baby Harry around, tickling him and cooing to him.

"You're lucky to have a brother," said Fatima as she munched on some potato salad. "It beats being an only child." Lee nodded in agreement.

"How so?" said Marvin, chewing on a hot dog.

"Well, you always have someone to play video games with, someone to tell secrets to, someone who will take sides with you against your parents . . ."

"Nah, all he does is cry and poop," said Marvin.

"That's all he does right now, knucklehead," Fatima said. "He's only a month old! He'll grow up. Then you'll have a built-in friend."

"That might not be so bad," said Marvin. "I don't know. He messed everything up so much when he arrived. But you're right—I guess I am lucky to have family."

Just then, Little Stevie Upton came out of the house, a cake in one hand, Amber Bluestone clutching the other. "Hey, Watson, why is your yard such a mess?"

"Yeah, you should really get that fence fixed," said Amber. "If you can afford it."

"How about something with iron spikes on it, to keep people like you two out?" Marvin said.

Marvin's mom turned her head. "Marvin!" she said. "I'm surprised at you. Be nice to your cousin."

"Hello, Aunt Mary," Little Stevie said.

Marvin's mom hoisted Baby Harry into a better position. "Harry, meet your cousin, Stevie," she said. Baby Harry clutched at the air with a tiny hand.

"Oh, look," said Amber. "He wants to shake hands."

"Hello, Harry," Stevie said, and gently shook the baby's hand.

"You have such good manners, Harry," Mrs. Watson said to the baby, jokingly.

"Yeah, it looks like you finally got it right this time," Little Stevie said. He glanced over at Marvin. "You know what they say—you always throw out the first draft."

Stevie handed the cake to Marvin. "Hold this, Watson," he said. Marvin glanced at the writing on the cake, which read *Better Luck with This One* in graceful script.

"Stevie, is your mother still out in the car?" Mrs. Watson asked.

"Yeah, you know her," said Little Stevie.

"Well, for heaven's sake! She hasn't eaten anything or even seen the baby yet! I'm being a terrible hostess." She turned to Marvin. "Marvin, help me take some food out to your aunt Constance. And grab that bag of canned goods so she can take them to the PLLA food drive." Marvin's mom was the president of the Pork Loaf Ladies' Auxiliary, PLI's charitable arm, but Little Stevie's mother had been acting as interim president while Mrs. Watson was on maternity leave.

Marvin filled up a paper plate with various potato and pasta salads, slaws, and grilled meats, and he followed his mother through the house, grabbing the grocery bag full of canned goods with his other hand. They went out front, where a long, black car was parked. Mrs. Watson rapped on the back door's tinted window, and it rolled down halfway to reveal Little Stevie's mom.

"Hello, Constance," said Mrs. Watson. "Thank you for coming. And the gift was so—thoughtful."

"Why, you're welcome, dear."

Marvin's mom glanced nervously at the locked car door. "Would you—would you like to come and join the party?"

"No, that's quite all right, dear. I'm perfectly fine here." The two women stared at each other in awkward silence. "It's not you," Constance Upton said. "It's this . . . *transitional* neighborhood."

Marvin looked around at his neighborhood. Across the street, an elderly couple rocked in matching chairs on their front porch. Down the way, kids were laughing and playing basketball. A small girl ran past, trying to get a kite aloft.

"I know you want to do good in this world, Mary, that you're always concerned about the less fortunate . . . but at what cost? I'll stay here in the car." Mrs. Upton rapped the window with her knuckles. "Bulletproof glass."

"Oh," said Mrs. Watson.

"And where's that new nephew of mine?" Constance asked. Marvin's mom hoisted Baby Harry to the opening so that her sister-in-law could give him a kiss on the forehead.

"We brought you something to eat, as well. Marvin?"

"Hello, Aunt Constance," Marvin said, holding the plate up to the half-open window. A Pork Loaf

Bratwurst rolled off the overloaded plate, smearing its tasty juices down the outside of the car door. Marvin quietly kicked it out of sight beneath the car.

"How sweet," said Mrs. Upton. "A doggie bag. But I'm afraid we had to put the dogs to sleep. It broke Little Stevie's heart."

"Sorry to hear that," Marvin said, still holding the plate awkwardly at the edge of the window. A trail of baked beans dribbled onto the glass.

"And how is school, young man?" she continued. "Stevie told me you were exposing yourself to your classmates. Is that correct?"

"Yeah, I guess so," Marvin said.

"Do you just careen from one fiasco to the next?" she asked, shaking her head.

"How do you mean?"

"Remember when you crashed your soapbox racer into my Rolls-Royce?" Constance asked, her eyebrow arching.

Marvin had built a car for a Soap Box Derby race a few years back. It was faster than anything else on the track—including Stevie's molded-fiberglass race car, which had been designed by PLI's Italian engineering division and tested in a NASA Jet Propulsion Laboratory wind tunnel for maximum aerodynamic efficiency. Marvin had saved on his car's weight by not installing a steering mechanism. Or brakes. He figured he could lean into the corners, and that the hill on the opposite end of the course would eventually bring him to a halt. But after he sailed off the track and through the crowd at the final turn, it was only the Upton family Rolls-Royce that had, fortunately, stopped him before he wound up in the river.

"Ever since then, I knew you were going to be a highly inventive and generally unsupervised boy," Constance said. She leaned in conspiratorially. "But don't tell your mother I said so. Poor dear does the best she can."

Marvin's mom, who was standing inches away, ground her heel into the asphalt and cleared her throat.

"Are you coming down with a cold, dear?" Constance asked, turning to Marvin's mom. "You should take care of yourself, especially with a new baby and a budding exhibitionist on your hands."

"Don't worry about me," Mrs. Watson said, forcing a smile. "Oh, I almost forgot," she added. "I have some things for you to take over to the canned food drive. Marvin, can you put that bag in the trunk?" Mrs. Upton nodded to the driver up front, who popped the trunk. Marvin, who was still holding the unwanted plate of barbecue, went around to the back of the car. He set the paper plate carefully into the mahogany-lined trunk, and then dropped the bag full of cans directly on top. Marvin shut the trunk firmly and gave the driver a smile and a thumbs-up.

"I hope the responsibilities at the Ladies' Auxiliary aren't too much for you and your busy schedule," Mrs. Watson said. "I didn't mean to put that all in your lap when the baby came."

"Oh, it's no trouble," Constance said, smiling. "You know how I love planning and organizing things. And when I stepped in, I could see that the PLLA certainly needs a *lot* of organizing."

"Does it," Mrs. Watson said coldly. "Well, it was lovely seeing you." She and Marvin then walked inside the house as the car window rolled shut behind them.

Back at the party, Marvin saw that Fatima was stewing in a quiet rage as Little Stevie and his date stood beside her and talked and talked.

"This is going to be a great year for me," said Little Stevie. "Not only am I going to be captain of the soccer team, but I have a strong feeling that Amber and I are going to be crowned king and queen of the Harvest Dance. They say no sixth grader has ever won before, but we'll change that, won't we?"

"It's in the bag, babe," Amber said.

"Oh yeah?" Fatima said angrily. Then she began furiously punching numbers into her wristwatch calculator. "Just a minute. Hold it. Hold that thought. Almost . . . nope, wait . . . *divide* by ten . . ."

"Um . . ." Little Stevie said.

"A-ha!" Fatima shouted. "Ahem. What I mean is, you're in for some competition."

"Oh, really?" said Little Stevie.

"That's right," said Fatima. "Marvin's taking me to the dance."

"He is?" said Little Stevie.

"I am?" said Marvin.

"Yes," said Fatima, elbowing Marvin in the ribs. She grinned through her headgear and laughed a fake, lighthearted laugh. "Just our little joke. Yes, Marvin's taking me, and we'll be entering the Harvest King and

Queen competition, too. We're going to give you a run for your money."

"You're going to have to run pretty fast to keep up with *our* money," said Amber Bluestone.

"That's big talk from a girl whose name is an oxymoron," said Fatima.

Amber got right up in Fatima's headgear. "*You're* the oxymoron!"

From the center of the yard, Uncle Steve called for everyone's attention, interrupting the confrontation. "Friends, neighbors, coworkers—I would like to propose a toast." He lifted high a plastic cup full of Pork Punch. "A toast to the newest member of the Upton-Watson clan: Harry Jr. May the apple fall far, far from the tree. Just kidding! Let me tell you a story about when I first met my brother-in-law, Harry Watson Sr. . . ."

As Uncle Steve droned on, Marvin leaned in close to Fatima and whispered, "What do you mean, I'm taking you to the dance?"

"Oh, don't get so wound up about it," said Fatima. "I calculated the likelihood that you would ask me to the dance—which was low—and calculated the likelihood that you would say no if I asked you—also low—and then I calculated that I should be spontaneous and seize the moment. So I did."

"But I don't really want to go to the dance," said Marvin.

"Look," she said. "I am *not* going to be shown up by your cousin. I refuse to let that pompous jerk win every honor at our school, just like he did at my last school. I am *going* to that dance, and *you're* taking me, and we're going to *win* those stupid crowns."

"But, we've never been on a date. How do you even know if you like me?" Marvin asked.

"Don't be naive," Fatima said. "Dating isn't about liking people."

"Well, what is it about, then?"

"Don't confuse the issue," she said. "I'll be wearing blue. Try not to clash."

"What color goes best with awkward?" Marvin asked. Fatima glared at him but didn't answer.

Interlude

A steam whistle cut through the night. In the moonlight, a long freight train rumbled across the sleepy countryside outside Butcherville toward its destination, PLI Meat-Processing Facility 44. The engineer knew the delivery was right on schedule. He prided himself on running his trains like clockwork. In exactly thirty-four minutes, he would drop off his cargo and be done for the night.

He blew the whistle again as the train approached a railroad crossing. Then, in the train's headlights, he saw a vehicle stopped in the middle of the tracks. The engineer, panicking, pulled the brake. The train screeched and shrieked as it ground to a halt, stopping just inches from the obstruction. Disaster averted, the engineer wiped the sweat from his forehead with trembling hands and climbed outside to see what had happened.

Parked on the tracks was a Volkswagen bus, painted black and white to look like a Holstein cow. The word "PorkPeace" was emblazoned across it. Surrounding the van were a dozen college-age kids, who were chanting, "Hey, hey! Ho, ho! P-L-I has got to go!" and "One, two, three, four! Don't eat cows anymore!"

"That's a terrible slogan," said the engineer.

The students stopped chanting, and one of them elbowed a tall, skinny youth who was wearing a T-shirt with a picture of Mr. Piggly Winks in the middle of a red circle with a slash through it. "I told you that was lame," said the first student.

"What's this all about?" asked the engineer. "You kids could have gotten yourselves killed."

"It would have been a small sacrifice to save the lives of those innocent cows," said the ringleader.

"Speak for yourself!" said a student in the back of the crowd.

"Well, I'm just glad nobody was hurt," said the engineer. "Now, do you mind moving your cow-van off the tracks so I can be on my way?"

"No can do. We're not moving this van until all those cows in your train are set free!"

"Set free? Are you crazy?" said the engineer. "Have you ever *seen* a stampede, son?"

"No, but I've seen the stampede of corporate greed that tramples this town every day!"

"Well, okay," said the engineer, shaking his head. He walked back to the cab of the engine and radioed the police.

Meanwhile, back in the long chain of cattle cars, all the cows were still peacefully asleep. All except for Bovina, or, as the plastic tag pinned to her ear indicated, Number 2378. She had restless bovine syndrome, which meant she slept lightly or not at all. Bovina noticed that the train had stopped, and she did not like it one bit. She chewed her cud uneasily and stared into the haunches of the cow in front of her.

Overhead, a hatch in the roof of the cattle car creaked open. With a shuffling noise, a dark shape filled the moonlit hatchway and then dropped into the car. A long, silvery line stretched down from the open hatch. Bovina heard a startled mooing from the front of the car, but couldn't see what was going on. The mooing stopped, and she watched as the dark shape scurried back up the line, with a much larger shape in tow. Again and again, the shape returned, pulling her herdmates from the car. Finally, she was the only one left.

"Moo!" Bovina called in alarm. She saw the shape descend once more, and she backed into the farthest corner of the train car.

"The ox hath therefore stretch'd his yoke in vain," said the shadowy shape. *"The ploughman lost his sweat, and the green corn hath rotted!"*

Sharp fangs plunged into Bovina's neck, and she suddenly felt much less restless. As she was hoisted into the air by a silver thread, she wondered what she had been so worried about, and fell into the first—and last—sound sleep of her life.

8

The Experiment

On Monday, Lee wobbled into the cafetorium, his shirt on backward. On his way to the lunch table, he bumped into three different students, two tables, and a wall. Finally, he settled himself into his seat across from Marvin. His eyes were glazed and unfocused.

"How you feeling, Lee?" Marvin asked.

"I've been better," Lee said.

"You actually don't smell so bad," Marvin said.

"That's great, but I sure am glad I don't have to keep this up much longer."

"You could try," said Fatima, who walked up to the table with her arms full of laboratory gear. "The human body can go without food for about sixty days. But it would make an interesting science experiment if you tried to break the record."

"That doesn't sound like a good idea," said Lee.

"You're right," said Fatima. "That would take too long; our results are due next week."

She turned to Marvin. "Here's some juicy gossip: I heard that Barry Walsh's dad got a speeding *ticket*."

"You don't say," Marvin said. "Does that really qualify as 'juicy'?"

Fatima looked at him for a long moment. "And you know what song I just love?" she said. " 'She's Got a TICKET to Ride,' by the Beatles."

"Um, yeah," Marvin said, raising his eyebrows. "That's great. But maybe we should talk about Lee and the experiment?"

"Absolutely," Fatima said. "When it comes to getting a good grade in our science lab, you could say that Lee is our meal *ticket*." She looked at Marvin expectantly.

"Stop saying 'ticket' already," Marvin said. "I bought the stupid tickets to the dance. They're burning a hole in my backpack. See?" He pulled them out and waved them in the air briefly.

"Well," she said, "I thought you might appreciate some subtle reminders. I didn't want to nag."

"Oh, I got my ticket, too," Lee said. He fumbled in his pockets for a few moments. "It's around here somewhere. I'm sure I could find it if I wasn't so dizzy."

"Have you really gone two days without eating?" Marvin asked.

"Thanks to Fatima, I was able to complete my task," said Lee. "I think Fatima is just great. So sweet and thoughtful."

"You really must not be feeling well," said Marvin.

"Yeah, I have been a little woozy," said Lee. "And I have been bumping into things a lot. But it's okay. Fatima watches over me."

"What the heck are you talking about?" Marvin asked, glancing from Lee to Fatima and back.

"I stopped by his house a few times to make sure he wasn't eating," Fatima said.

"My grandmother said she doesn't know if she likes you watching me through binoculars," said Lee. "But I still think you're the best."

"You spied on him through binoculars?" Marvin asked.

"In case I needed to intervene," she said.

"What do you mean, 'intervene'?"

"Well, at one point, I had to sneak into his house and scrape the food off his dinner plate when his grandmother wasn't looking," she said.

"How did you manage that?"

"It wasn't easy," she said. "It involved three broken windows and a ten-foot-long squeegee. But the important thing is, the integrity of the experiment has been preserved. Now, let's get to work." Fatima spread out her gear: notepad, pencil, digital camera, toothpicks, tape measure, empty plastic sandwich bags, and other odds and ends.

"What's all that for?" Marvin asked.

"We need to follow the scientific method, per Miss Sweeney's instructions," Fatima said. She reached across and grabbed Lee's lunch bag, emptying its contents onto the table.

"I thought we'd just shove some food in his mouth and see what happens," Marvin said. "That's how I get *my* science on."

"So you're a *mad* scientist, is that it?" Fatima said, scowling.

"Well, I don't have a mountaintop fortress with a

death ray, or anything—not for lack of trying, mind you—"

"We need to be methodical in the way we conduct this experiment," Fatima said. "Science and reckless-ness don't mix."

"Look around you at the miracle of life, Fatima," Marvin said. "Stars and galaxies spinning through the depths of space. Majestic mountains and sweeping plains teeming with plants and animals. The Pork Loaf Big 'Un, making everyone in a ten-foot radius salivate like a drooling baby! Do you think all that came about thanks to tape measures and toothpicks and careful notes?"

"The Big 'Un is not a miracle of life," Fatima said.

"Big 'Un . . ." Lee muttered through the haze of his hunger. "Oh, you're so wrong. I'd trade both of you for a Big 'Un right now."

Marvin looked back at Fatima and said, "I just think the fundamental secrets of the universe are *not that boring.*"

"I did not imply that anything was boring, only orderly and rational," Fatima said. "The universe holds itself together with laws and rules, and our job as young scientists is to uncover, catalogue, and appreciate those laws. There's nothing boring about that." Lee groaned in hunger and disagreement. "Now can we get on with this?" she continued. "Before Lee eats one of our arms?" She turned to their test subject. "First, we need to document all the food in your typical diet," Fatima said. She unwrapped Lee's sandwich. "Is this your usual lunch?"

Lee nodded. "My grandmother makes me a Pork Loaf sandwich every day."

Fatima picked up a knife from her lunch tray and began slicing Lee's sandwich into little pieces. She put small squares of each component—bread, cheese, tomato, Pork Loaf, and so on—into separate plastic bags and then photographed each one with her digital camera.

"Now, we start reintroducing Lee to food," she said.

Marvin poked a cube of bread with a toothpick. He waved it in front of Lee's face. "Hello, Lee, this is food! Hello, food, this is Lee!"

"Just give me the food!" said Lee.

"No, wait!" Fatima said sharply. "Don't give it to him yet. We haven't established a baseline."

"What baseline?" asked Marvin.

"His baseline smelliness!" Fatima said.

"How do we measure that?" Marvin asked.

"Here, I'll show you." Fatima looked out into the aisle at a student who was passing by. "You, there! Volunteer!"

The student stopped. "Who, me?" he asked.

"How close would you stand to this boy?" She grabbed him by the elbow and shoved him right up next to Lee. "Is that close enough for you?"

"Yes, plenty close, thanks," said the student. "Can I go now?"

"Not yet," Fatima said. "Marvin—measure how far away he is from Lee and record it." She slapped a tape measure into Marvin's hand.

Marvin stretched the tape out between the subject and the volunteer. "Eight inches," he said, then scribbled it down on the notepad.

"Thank you for your participation," Fatima said, shoving the student back out into the aisle. "Now leave. Results will be published in due time."

Fatima coerced several more passersby into volunteering, and Marvin measured and tallied the results.

In Lee's non-smelly state, people stood an average distance of twelve and a half inches away from him.

Meanwhile, as volunteer after volunteer was caught and released, Lee's mouth was opening wider and wider with every passing minute. He stared at the cubes of sandwich parts spread out before him with a frantic look in his eyes. "Oh, feed me!" he finally cried. "Feed me! Feed me!"

"Can I feed him now?" Marvin asked Fatima.

"All right," she said. "Go ahead."

Marvin popped the cube of bread into Lee's watering mouth. "Oh, food, glorious food!" Lee said as he munched. "White bread never tasted so good."

They waited sixty seconds for any odor to surface, figuring that might be enough time. They noticed nothing. Fatima grabbed another student, and Marvin diligently measured the distance between Lee and the volunteer. "No change," Fatima said. "Move on to the tomato."

Marvin picked up a cube of tomato and dropped it onto Lee's tongue. "Truly, this is the finest tomato," Lee said. "The most juicy, the most flavorful, the most wonderful tomato that I've ever eaten!"

Again they measured the distance at which volunteers would be willing to stand next to Lee, and again there was no change. It was the same with the cheese, the lettuce, and the pickles.

"Nothing," Marvin said. The only ingredient left on the table was a mound of pink cubes of Pork Loaf.

"Of course," said Fatima. "By process of elimination, it must be the Pork Loaf. We've gotten no reaction from the previous five ingredients. We don't even need to test it."

"But is that *scientific*?" Marvin asked. "Seems kind of *reckless*."

Fatima rolled her eyes at him. "Thank you for pointing that out, Marvin. No, it's *not* scientific. We should actually test it."

"For science!" shouted Lee, stabbing a Pork Loaf cube with a toothpick and plunging the meat into his open mouth.

All was still as Lee chewed and chewed and chewed at the lump of luncheon meat. The seconds ticked by, and there was no reaction.

Fifteen seconds.

Lee swallowed.

Thirty seconds.

"Anything?" Fatima asked, squinting at Lee.

"I feel fine," Lee said, already eyeing the rest of his dismembered sandwich.

Forty-five seconds.

Marvin glanced at Fatima. "Well, I guess you were wrong, Fatima."

"Time's not up yet," she said. "We need to wait a full minute if we're going to be *scientific*."

Fifty-nine seconds.

"So much for your theory," Marvin said to Fatima. "I guess it's not the—"

Just then, the cafetorium lights seemed to flicker and dim. Lee's stomach gave out a low rumble.

"Guys? Guys?" said Lee. "Something's happening . . ."

Fatima pulled out a pair of swimmer's nose clips, snapped them into place, and ducked down, hugging her knees as though she were assuming an airline crash position.

As Marvin turned his head toward Lee, the stench rolled out from his lab partner like a sonic boom. It hit Marvin full in the face—a hot, dense, humid

wind carrying the scents of a summer fish market and long-forgotten gym socks. The odor was a force of nature, like a hurricane or an erupting volcano. It overwhelmed the senses and made Marvin long for the comparatively tame smell of his baby brother's diapers. He toppled backward out of his seat as though he had been slapped.

The wave spread out from Lee like ripples in a pond. The other schoolchildren, struck by the smell, tried to flee but were knocked down. They clawed and climbed and overturned tables in their haste to escape. The lunch ladies yelped and abandoned their posts. In short order, the entire population of the cafetorium was standing in a wide, clearly defined circle with Lee at its center—the boundary at which his odor was tolerable.

Marvin, still on the floor, began to crawl for the safety of that boundary.

"No! Measure! Measure!" Fatima cried in a nasal voice. Marvin groaned and turned around. He hooked the end of the tape measure into the collar of Lee's shirt and ran as fast as he could for the nauseated crowd. But he was brought up short, with a sudden jerk, several feet from the nearest student.

"Well?" asked Fatima. "What's the distance?"

"I don't know," Marvin said. "This is only a twelve-foot tape measure. It's not long enough."

"Do I have to do everything myself?" She walked over to where Marvin stood, marked the end of the tape measure on the floor with a pencil, and then measured the distance from that spot to the edge of the crowd. "There—eighteen feet, two inches."

The other students glared at Marvin and Fatima, clearly looking for some explanation. "My mom *told* me those hard-boiled eggs had gone bad," Marvin said, shaking his head in mock regret, "but I didn't listen to her." Gradually, the smell began to weaken. Marvin and Fatima left the angry, muttering crowd and made their way back to the table.

"How about that," Marvin said as he sat down. "It *was* the Pork Loaf, after all."

Fatima pulled off her nose clips and glared at him. "I hate you."

"Wait a minute," Marvin said, suddenly troubled

by the implications of their experiment. "Does this mean that there's something wrong with Pork Loaf?"

"My hypothesis has *always* been that there's something wrong with Pork Loaf," said Fatima. "And here's our first evidence." She pointed at Lee.

"I don't like the sound of that," Lee said. They all stared with suspicion and dread at the cubes of Pork Loaf piled on the table.

"Can I eat the rest of my sandwich now?" Lee asked.

Interlude

Another day at the zoo was ending, and the elephant's keepers were gently herding him into his enclosure for the night. On any other day he would have put up a fuss, but today he was feeling a bit wistful and went quietly. Earlier, a small girl had tried to pass a hot dog to him, which had reminded him of the good old days at the Bronx Zoo, where he was born. He ran with a fast herd there, always getting into scraps with the other bulls. Now here he was serving out his remaining years stuck in this small-town zoo. The town was so boring that he was starting to forget things, which was pretty bad for an elephant. He had almost forgotten what a hot dog tasted like. The girl had pushed the dog between the bars in an attempt to give it to him. It was the perfect frank, with mustard and green relish, just the way he liked it. They didn't serve much in this town besides Pork Loaf, so a real hot dog was a rare sight.

But just as he reached over with his trunk to seize the delightful snack, the girl's mother jerked the food away, admonishing her child: "Elephants don't eat hot dogs!"

The elephant had let out a snort to indicate that, yes, indeed, he *did* eat hot dogs, but the family had already turned away. He felt a wave of melancholy that started in his flapping ears and washed all the way down to his large, padded feet.

He was still feeling that melancholy when one of the zookeepers called out to him. "Come on, Big 'Un—time for bed." As the final aspect of his humiliation, after they had transferred him from the Bronx to the PLI Zoo and Aquarium, they had renamed him Big 'Un, after the Pork Loaf product. At least it was better than being named Pork Punch, which is what they called the chattering colobus monkey across the way. But no matter what they called the elephant, he would never forget that his real name was Bruno.

As the zookeepers latched his cell door shut, the nearby animals began to act up. The baboons, Lovable and Loafable (after the Pork Loaf "Lovable Loafables" lunch packs), were howling and climbing up and down the rope ladders in their cage. Log Roll, the elderly lion, was pacing back and forth, shaking his patchy mane and growling softly, while the giraffe, Pork Slims, was inexplicably pawing at the wall with his hooves.

"Whoa, easy there, Slims," said the senior zoo-keeper. "You just simmer down, now. Ain't nothing to worry about in here. No more kids throwing peanuts at your head today. Just get yourself some shut-eye."

"Boy, they're all really agitated," said the junior zookeeper.

"Must be a storm coming," his boss said. They turned off the lights and shut the outside door behind them as they left.

Bruno settled himself down to sleep. Outside his cell, the other animals were still chattering and roar-ing. But it was all right—the noise reminded Bruno of the hubbub of New York City. He was just closing his eyes, preparing to dream of the old neighborhood, when Log Roll let out an exceptionally loud roar. Bruno hoisted his head up and looked across the way to see a large, shadowy shape in the cage with the lion, back-ing the old, toothless animal into a corner. Log Roll unsheathed his claws—which were still sharp, despite his age—and leaped at the threatening shape. But his opponent was too quick and dodged to the side, sending the lion crashing into the bars with a loud clatter.

The old cat lay there in an exhausted heap, breathing heavily as the shadowy shape closed in for the kill.

Bruno had seen enough. He got back to his feet, strode over to the door, and reached through the bars with his trunk to unlatch his cage—something his dim-witted keepers never suspected he was capable of. Bruno flung open the door and let out a mighty bellow that shook the walls and stopped the dark menace in its tracks.

"Ah!" said the monster, scuttling out the door of the lion's cage. "At last, an opponent who can stand against me." As the creature stepped into the moonlight, Bruno could finally see his enemy for what it was.

It was a spider. An *enormous* spider.

The spider's body and legs were covered with bristling hairs, like an angry push broom. His many eyes gleamed and glistened with reflected light. His fangs were—strangely unimpressive. In fact, even though the creature was the size of a horse, it seemed tiny next to Bruno. The elephant wasn't worried.

Bruno swung his trunk in a wide circle and smacked the spider into a wall. The spider let out a surprised shriek, then laughed as he regained his footing.

"What, lost in the labyrinth of thy fury!" the spider cried out. *"Shall the elephant carry it thus? He beats me, and I rail at him: O worthy satisfaction!"* He let loose a fearsome battle cry, and reared back on four of his legs. "Alas, that your mighty strength will be no match for my knowledge of the arts of combat." The spider's four front limbs spun around his head in geometric patterns unknown to man or elephant, whirring as they arced through the air in a strangely mesmerizing way that foretold death.

Bruno, tired of his opponent's nonsense, grabbed one of the spider's spinning legs with his trunk and yanked it off.

The spider screamed in pain. *He comes apart pretty easily for such a bigmouth,* Bruno thought.

The many-eyed monster backed into a corner, nursing his wound. *Time to squash this spider,* Bruno decided. He flexed his mighty legs and charged.

He steadily built up speed, his legs propelling him forward, his head bent down, his tusks out, the full

weight of his massive body moving toward his foe like an unstoppable freight train.

But at the last moment, the spider zipped up a nearly invisible silken thread to the ceiling, leaving Bruno to crash headlong into the concrete wall, knocking himself unconscious.

"My dancing soul doth celebrate this feast of battle with mine adversary," the spider said as he descended his silver cord, settling onto the elephant's motionless body. "In other words, chow time!"

9

The Stench

On Tuesday of the week following the lunchroom experiment, Marvin retired to his attic bedroom after school to do homework. He unzipped his backpack and pulled out his textbooks and notebooks. As he did so, a small, forgotten envelope fluttered to the floor. Marvin looked at it for a moment, then picked it up gingerly, as he might handle a bad report card he had to bring home to his parents. Or nuclear waste. In either case, you didn't really want to touch it, but you were afraid of what might happen if you lost it. So it was with this envelope, which contained the tickets to the Harvest Dance. He let out a long sigh, then placed the envelope in the top drawer of his dresser. Marvin distractedly worked on his algebra problems for a few minutes, unable to take his mind off the approaching dance, before his mom called him down to dinner.

The next morning, Marvin ran into Lee just

outside their science class. It was the day of the big demonstration.

"Good morning, Marvin!" Lee said brightly. "Isn't it an amazing day to be alive?"

"Hey, Lee," Marvin said. "Why are you blowing sunshine up my shorts?"

"I feel great!" Lee said, a wide grin on his face. "All the fasting I've had to do for this experiment has brought me a new clarity of mind. I feel like I'm reaching a higher level of spiritual awareness."

"You don't say," Marvin said.

"Plus, I don't smell!" Lee said. "It's incredible!"

"Well, after today, you won't ever have to eat Pork Loaf again if you don't want to," Marvin said.

"Yeah, that's the only problem," Lee said. "My grandmother's really mad that I refuse to eat Pork Loaf at dinner. I told her it was for my education, but she didn't believe me. So last night she made me scrub the floor with a toothbrush."

"That's a bummer," Marvin said.

"Yeah," Lee said. "But you know, doing humble work like that really opens your eyes and makes you think about your place in the wider world." He paused.

"Of course, it wasn't so great later, when I had to brush my teeth."

They went into the science lab and sat down near Fatima, who was going over the notes for their presentation. The bell rang, and Miss Sweeney stood up in front of the class.

"Who would like to talk about their experiment?" Miss Sweeney asked. "Do we have a volunteer to go first?"

Fatima's hand shot into the air. "Ooh! Ooh!" she cried, waving her arm frantically. No one else's hand was up.

"Amber?" the teacher said, looking right past Fatima. "Is your team ready?"

"Yes, Miss Sweeney, we're fully prepared," Amber Bluestone said, smiling. Amber and Stevie went up to the front of the room, and Roland Offenbach brought up the rear, carrying a large piece of foam-core poster-board and a plastic bread bag.

Fatima, attempting to hide her irritation, said, "No worries, guys—you always have a warm-up act before the main event."

Roland placed the foam-core board on an easel at the front of the room and set the bag of bread on a lab table. He stood to the side with his arms folded and looked menacing. It was his natural state.

Amber stood beside the poster, smiling, and gestured at the words written there as if she were a model at a boat show. The board read:

OUR SCIENCE EXPERIMENT:
"THIS BREAD IS MOLDY"

Our Blue-Ribbon Team:
Amber Bluestone, Stephen Upton Jr.,
Roland Offenbach

Suggested Grade: A++

In the center of the board was a crudely drawn outline of a slice of bread with a question mark in the middle.

Stevie slowly paced back and forth in the front of the room, stroking his chin as if deep in thought, then began his speech.

"What leads man to explore the limits of the universe?" he asked. "To question the status quo, the natural world, indeed, the very fabric of our reality, and ask: 'Why is stuff like that?' "

Stevie's classmates—with the exception of Lee, Marvin, and Fatima—were rapt. Stevie continued. "Like Newton and Einstein before us, we, too, sought to slake an unquenchable thirst for knowledge. A burning thirst nurtured by our own Miss Sweeney." Stevie gestured to Miss Sweeney, who smiled and blushed a little. "So without further ado—say it with me, now—THIS . . . BREAD . . . IS . . . MOLDY!" The class shouted the words along with him and cheered. "Roland!" Stevie said, turning to his teammate. "The bread!"

Roland, apparently unable to work a twist tie, simply tore the bag open and removed a slice of moldy bread. He walked over to the easel and stuck the bread to the foam-core board with a pin.

Stevie aimed a laser pointer at the bread. "We found several different strains of mold," he said, pointing first to a patch of blue mold. "Over here you see *Moldus Blueus*—to use the Latin—and over here is some *Moldus Greenus*. And lastly, the most elusive of all, *Moldus Whiteus*." He aimed the red laser dot at a furry blotch that was nearly the same color as the bread itself.

Miss Sweeney stood up and clapped wildly. "Wonderful! Just wonderful!" she said, beaming. "Maybe you could tell us a little bit more about how you conducted your experiment."

"Yes, certainly," Stevie said. "Good question!"

"We left the bag in Roland's locker over the weekend," Amber said. She gestured to the bread and smiled, showing off her perfect teeth. "And you can see the results!"

Stevie nodded soberly. "That's right," he said. "Using observation, and the power of thinking, we *knew* it would get moldy. *That* was our insight."

Fatima asked, "Were you trying to grow penicillin?"

Amber frowned. "What's penicillin?"

"Hmm," Stevie said. "A good question, Amber. Indeed, what *is* penicillin? But I'm afraid that a thorough discussion of such a weighty scientific mystery is beyond the scope of today's presentation." He bowed. "Thank you all for your time! Good night!"

Miss Sweeney began clapping again, and Roland walked back through the rows of desks, shouting and hooting, "Give it up! Ooh! Ooh! Ooh!" The class clapped and cheered.

"We're next! We're next!" Fatima shouted, running to set up their presentation. She connected her laptop to a projector and called up the first slide:

An investigation into the cause of negative olfactory stimulation by a young adult male subject, age 12 years.

Lee sat facing the class in a chair at the front of the room, and Marvin stood beside him. Fatima clicked to the next slide. It was a photograph of Lee with a black bar over his eyes. The caption read, *Anonymous Subject, L.S.*

Lee craned his neck around to look at the slide and then leaned over to whisper to Marvin. "Is that me? He has the same initials as me."

Fatima cleared her throat. "Upon interviewing Subject L.S., our team formulated an initial hypothesis that the subject's condition—an odoriferous emanation similar to putrefaction—was not endemic, but rather the result of a foreign agent."

Someone in the class called out, "You mean a spy?"

Fatima ignored the question and continued. "Subsequent testing revealed that the causative agent was in fact a porcine-derived edible substance. The research process that brought us to this conclusion is the subject of our presentation today."

The class looked befuddled.

"Speak American!" Roland shouted.

Miss Sweeney stood up. "Now, Fatima, if you don't have any findings, you don't need to try to dress up your experiment with fancy language. You could take a lesson from Amber's team."

Marvin cut in. "Oh, we have findings," he said, earning an irritated look from Fatima. "In fact, we'll demonstrate them now." He picked up a tray of food from the lab table.

"As I'm sure you've all noticed, Lee has . . . an odor," Marvin said. Two dozen heads nodded. "In our experiment, we decided to find out what causes this odor. We quickly eliminated personal hygiene as a factor. Lee showers every day and has worn deodorant since he was five."

"I also wear this baking soda charm!" Lee said,

pulling from his shirt a necklace on which a linen sachet hung.

"Exactly," Marvin said. He turned to the class. "So, what else could have caused this smell?"

"Does he never wash his clothes?" someone shouted.

"Does he have moldy cheese in his pockets?"

"Does he live in a barn?"

"Does he ride to school in a garbage truck?"

"Does he have a pet skunk?"

"Does he dabble in the dark arts?"

"What? The dark arts? No!" said Fatima. "Are you insane? This is science class."

The last questioner mumbled to himself grumpily, "Well, he smells like he's haunted."

"Does he have a fungus?"

"Yeah, athlete's butt," said Stevie, to general laughter.

"Does he have—um—digestive problems?" someone in the back asked.

"Yes!" Marvin cried, pointing to the questioner. "We hypothesized that he might be allergic to something in his diet. So, we first had him fast, in order to clean out his system, and then reintroduced different foods under controlled conditions. Observe."

Marvin stabbed a cube of white bread with a toothpick and popped it into Lee's open mouth. Fatima clicked a stopwatch to begin timing the 60-second observation period. At the end of a long minute, she clicked it again, and nodded to Marvin.

"As you can tell," Marvin said to the class, "there is no significant odor change. So we were able to eliminate the bread."

Marvin went through each of the sandwich items one by one, as the class grew increasingly bored and irritated.

"What is this, a buffet?" one of the kids finally screamed. "Get on with it, already!" Everyone muttered and grumbled in agreement, including Miss Sweeney.

"All right . . ." Marvin said, and he and Fatima began to suit up. They clamped nose clips in place, and pulled on safety goggles as well as full plastic face shields. They stepped into white disposable hazmat suits and donned heavy rubber gloves. Fatima—with her thick glasses beneath her safety goggles and face shield, and her pinched-shut nose above her formidable headgear—looked even more awkward than usual.

She turned to face the class, beaming with excitement. "Now," she said in a ridiculous nasal voice through her nose clip, "as you can see, we've come to the last and most crucial ingredient." She gestured with her gloved hands, squeaking with every movement. "Allow me to demonstrate—"

"That's an improvement on your usual look, Fatima," Stevie yelled, interrupting. "Maybe you could do us all a favor and complete the ensemble by putting a bag over your head."

The room erupted in laughter and Fatima's face paled. "I—I—" she stammered amid the guffawing, too shocked to continue, too embarrassed to think of any comeback. She turned with a squeak of metal and looked to Marvin for help.

Marvin narrowed his eyes. *He* could think of a comeback.

On an impulse, he grabbed the plate of Pork Loaf cubes and, instead of placing just one into Lee's mouth, shoveled them all in at once. Lee's eyes opened wide and he gagged on a muffled gasp of protest.

Fatima turned to Marvin as she realized what he was doing. "No, wait . . . !" she said, too late to stop him.

Marvin turned back to her and shouted above the noise of the laughter, commanding, "Start the timer." Fatima fumbled for her stopwatch and clicked it. Miss Sweeney shook her head in irritation and jotted down notes in her grade book.

As the seconds ticked away and Lee swallowed his last gulp of Pork Loaf amid hoots and catcalls from the audience, Marvin strode across the front of the room and grabbed Fatima's elbow, bringing her along with him as he ducked behind the safety of a lab table.

"I don't think you should have done that," Fatima said to Marvin in a shaky voice.

"No one ever broke new ground without taking risks," Marvin said.

Lee shifted uncomfortably in his chair. Beads of sweat were forming on his forehead. His cheeks turned rosy. "I've never eaten so much Pork Loaf so quickly," Lee said. "I don't feel so good." His eyes glazed over, and a low moan escaped his lips.

"Thirty seconds!" Fatima shouted from behind the lab desk.

On the windowsill, the classroom's pet hamster, Sorbet, began running frantically in its exercise wheel. The birds in the bushes just outside the window squawked in alarm and flew away. Marvin felt the hair standing up on his arms, as though an electric charge was building in the air.

"Forty seconds!" Fatima said.

"I can't breathe," Lee said, pulling at his collar. All his exposed skin had a distinctive reddish tinge now. His shirt was drenched with sweat.

"Is it getting hot in here?" Miss Sweeney asked as the students' laughter died down. Indeed, the temperature in the entire room seemed to be rising. A faint shimmering haze, the kind you see above asphalt on a hot summer day, was visible above Lee's head. The paint on the wall behind his chair began to blister and peel. In an ever-widening circle with Lee at its center, the linoleum tiles on the floor buckled and curled.

"This is a totally uncontrolled experiment," Fatima said. "I ran computer simulations, but not for a quantity of Pork Loaf this large. The rate of absorption into his bloodstream has to be astronomical. If his body can't buffer the reaction, there are going to be serious—"

"Fifty seconds!" Marvin said. "Get down!"

Lee was slouched down in his chair, his head rolling backward, his breath coming in short gasps. Suddenly, he opened his eyes and sat bolt-upright. He opened his mouth as if to say something.

From the back of the room, Little Stevie called out, "This is the lamest thing that I've ever—"

His next words were entirely drowned out by the thunderclap.

The windows of the classroom blew outward, glass shattering across the yard. Throughout the room, lab beakers and test tubes cracked under the strain. Desks, chairs, and children were thrown violently backward as if they were bowling pins. Miss Sweeney, in her rolling desk chair, was slammed into the wall. The gooseneck lab faucets were torn free, sending gouts of water into the air.

As the boom passed, the stench settled in. Students began to gag and cough and stumble blindly out of the rubble. Amber Bluestone cried out, "My eyes are burning!" and ran into the emergency chemical shower. At first, kids leaned their heads out the shattered windows to get some fresh air, but it quickly turned into a mad stampede as one after another climbed out to safety.

A student came running down the hallway to investigate the noise and drew back visibly at the smell. "There's a gas leak in the science lab!" he cried, and pulled a nearby fire alarm.

As the alarm rang out, Marvin's remaining classmates ran from the room. He stood up and shouted to Stevie, who was one of the last to leave, "Hey, genius! Don't forget your moldy bread!"

With the assistance of the firefighters, Marvin and Fatima moved Lee and the still-dizzy Miss Sweeney out to the lawn, where the rest of the student body stood in neat rows, lined up by classroom as they had been taught in their fire drills. Lee was disoriented, with signs of a concussion, but the EMTs were finding it difficult to treat him, as his odor had never been stronger. Finally, one of the firemen was able to tend to him, while equipped with a face mask and oxygen tank.

The rest of Marvin's science class had been ushered into a hastily erected quarantine tent, intended for use in case of large-scale chemical spills or biological hazards. They were being run through decontamination procedures in an effort to eradicate the smell that Lee's eruption had saturated them with.

Fatima's glasses were cracked, despite the safety goggles and face shield she had been wearing, but she was otherwise unhurt. Neither she nor Marvin had been left stinky by the explosion, thanks to their full-body safety gear. She squinted over in the direction of Miss Sweeney, who was laid out on a stretcher, being examined by the EMTs.

"I hope she's all right," Fatima said. "That definitely deserved an A."

The rescue crews and school administrators stood off to one side, conferring in hushed tones. The principal wore a look of panic on his face.

At last, the firefighters got Lee to his feet. The fireman in the respirator walked away, taking off his mask. He was an older fellow with a bushy, graying mustache.

"I don't know why we're here taking care of a bunch of smelly kids and some fire alarm prank," he said to a younger fireman as they passed Marvin and Fatima. "Not with what's going on over at the zoo."

"I heard they might be calling in the FBI," said the young guy. "Or maybe even the National Guard." The older man suddenly noticed Marvin and Fatima watching them, and elbowed his partner to be quiet. They climbed into their fire engine and drove off.

"The zoo?" Marvin asked Fatima. She shrugged.

To everyone's surprise, the students were not sent back to class. They were sent home, without explanation.

The Uptons' driver pulled up in a black car and got out to open the door for Little Stevie and Amber.

"Your ride home, si—" the driver began but involuntarily gagged at the smell of them. He stepped back a few feet while they climbed in, and then put up the partition to separate the front seat from the passengers.

Everyone else lined up at the hurriedly organized buses or else made their way home on foot. Marvin and Fatima walked the still-woozy Lee home, as the driver wouldn't let him on the bus, and they weren't sure he would be able to make it on his own. The streets were strangely empty, and they passed the trip in silence.

When at last they arrived at Lee's doorstep, Marvin clapped him on the back and said, "Good job today, Lee."

"Shove it, Marvin," Lee said.

"What?" Marvin said.

Lee turned to face him. His hair was sweaty and disheveled, and his skin was still blotchy. "I know this is just some sort of joke to you, but I was actually smelling better. Now I smell so bad, even *I* can't stand it."

"Hey, I'm sorry, Lee," Marvin said. "It was all in the name of science."

Lee snorted. "I saw what happened. You did this to me just so you could get back at your cousin."

"Now, wait a minute—" Marvin began.

"And whatever's going on between *you two*," Lee said, pointing back and forth at Marvin and Fatima, "leave me out of it." He went inside and slammed the door shut.

Marvin turned to Fatima, still stunned. "Going on between us? I don't know what he's talking about," he said. "Do *you* know what he's talking about?"

Fatima said nothing for a minute, then took off her broken glasses and squinted at them. "I don't know if I can find my way home with my glasses like this," she said. "Can you walk me back?"

Marvin realized it was the first time he had seen her without her glasses on. For a moment, she ceased to be Fatima, the all-knowing, bossy supernerd who caused him such aggravation. Instead, he saw just a girl who had broken her glasses and needed some help.

He nodded and then, afraid she wouldn't be able to see the gesture, added, "Sure."

They walked to Fatima's house along silent streets, accompanied only by the rustling of the first autumn leaves. Not even the sound of a squirrel or bird could be heard. Although the sky was bright and blue, it felt to Marvin like a storm was coming.

10

The Panic

Marvin went upstairs as soon as he got home, glad for the few extra hours of free time. His mother was out with Harry Jr. at a mother–baby yoga class, so Marvin was going to be stuck with either his dad's cooking or a bowl of cereal. He opted for the Cinnamon Frosted Pork Puffs and went upstairs. He was looking forward to some peace.

As he opened his bedroom door, a lukewarm liquid cascaded down on his head, followed by a metal bucket, which struck with a painful clank.

"Our perimeter's been breached!" a voice shouted. Marvin immediately found himself being pummeled by attackers he couldn't see through the drenching liquid. They beat him back, driving him out onto the landing before slamming the door shut and turning the lock. Marvin stood there, stunned, smelling faintly of vinegar. Unbidden, he heard the word "shower-kraut" ringing in his head, but the liquid with which he had been doused instead appeared to be some sort of mildly warm vinaigrette. Apparently, his middle school years were destined to be preserved in his memories by—well—preservatives. He wiped off his face and then banged on the door.

"Hey!" he shouted. "Whoever you are, get out of my room!"

He could hear shuffling from behind the door. Someone fiddled with the latch. The door opened a crack, and Marvin was greeted with another deluge of salad dressing before it slammed shut again.

"Hey!" he sputtered, spitting the dressing out of his mouth. "What's the big idea?"

"He's still there," a voice whispered. "I told you the oil wasn't hot enough!"

"Could you come back in ten minutes?" another voice called out. "We need time to boil more oil."

"What?" Marvin asked.

"If you're not with us, you're against us!" the voice called back through the door.

"That doesn't make any sense, and you're in *my* room," Marvin said. "Open up!"

There was a momentary silence from the other side of the door. Then a voice whispered, "Okay. Just . . . don't . . . move . . ."

At that, the door opened a crack, and a wooden spoon came swinging down through the narrow space, whacking Marvin in the head repeatedly.

"Ow!" Marvin cried. "Quit it!" He seized the spoon in the middle of its downward arc and wrenched it from his attacker's hand. Then he forced the door open, flailing the spoon before him.

"Retreat! Retreat!" the attackers shouted, and Marvin quickly saw that it was Abraham, Aristotle, and Ahab who had been holding the door against him. They fled to the far side of the room, the two smaller moths hiding behind Ahab's great bulk. Ahab wielded several slotted spoons and spatulas in his many hands. He also wore an old apron whose pockets were overflowing with armaments. The apron read, "Kiss the cook," but one of the moths had scrawled *OF DEATH!* after the other words.

"Oh, it's just that weird kid," said Abraham at last. He stepped out from behind Ahab. "What do you want, kid?"

"This is my room!" Marvin said.

"Is it?" Aristotle said. "Property rights are typically suspended during wartime. I don't think you can really say this is 'your' room, any more than I can say that it's my room. It's been annexed to serve the collective good."

"The needs of the many outweigh the needs of weird little boys who come in unannounced and trip our booby traps," said Abraham. "Leaving us defenseless against intruders."

"You doused me in salad dressing!" Marvin said.

"Sorry, that wasn't the plan," said Abraham. "It was *supposed* to be boiling oil. If a certain moth"—he jerked his head in the direction of Ahab, whose head drooped in shame—"hadn't scrounged up a *broken* hot plate from the next attic over, we would have scalded the flesh right off of you."

"Apology accepted, I guess," Marvin said. "But what are you doing here? Why aren't you in your own attic?"

"Because of the Elephant Vampire, of course!" Abraham said. "We were watching TV when the news broke. Then we thought we heard something that sounded just like an Elephant Vampire coming from the other end of our attic. So we barricaded ourselves in here." He waved an arm at a mound of debris that had been shoved into the hole in the wall.

"You did what?" Marvin said, taking in the mess. "You did what to my room?"

"I really think that such questions in this time of crisis are unpatriotic," Abraham said.

"I don't know what that even means," Marvin said. "And what the heck is an Elephant Vampire?"

"I'll fill you in, my young recruit," Aristotle said, taking Marvin by the elbow and walking him toward the far side of the attic.

"This is the war room," the moth said.

"You mean, just this corner?" Marvin asked.

"Yes," Aristotle said, stopping in front of a bulletin board. "Stand up straight and pay attention as I guide you through your security briefing." He first pointed to a clipping of a newspaper story—apparently stolen from one of the neighbor's porches—whose headline read: ELEPHANT VAMPIRE STRIKES BUTCHERVILLE! MAYOR DECLARES STATE OF EMERGENCY AND FEAR!

Below the headline was an infographic describing the basic facts:

- Animals had been going missing for many days.
- That morning, the skin and bones of the beloved elephant, Big 'Un, had been found at the zoo.
- The elephant's insides had been sucked out.
- A dusk-to-dawn curfew was in effect until further notice.

"Wow," said Marvin. "They sure got these newspapers out fast."

"Who says print is dead?" Aristotle said. "Unfortunately, the paperboy probably *is* dead, what with the Elephant Vampire on the loose. Experts such as myself theorize that the creature first dined on smaller animals around town, growing larger day by day. And now that it is full grown, it has taken to its natural prey: elephants." The tall moth pointed to a drawing of Dumbo, apparently ripped from an old children's book.

Marvin's eyes wandered from the cartoon elephant to the other objects pinned to the cluttered war room wall. "What's the rest of this stuff?" he asked.

"This is how we plan our strategy and keep track of

the enemy's movements. Here"—he pointed to a cartoon map of Butcherville that was clearly an old place mat from a fast-food restaurant—"we have plotted the locations of all of the recent animal disappearances and confirmed kills." The map was covered with stickers of animals as well as pushpins that were connected to one another with yarn. "Here we see where a junkyard dog vanished. And over here, a significant drop in local alley cat population. And this cheeseburger"—he pointed to a sticker shaped like a smiling cheeseburger—"represents a rail car full of missing cows." He turned to Marvin sheepishly. "We didn't have a cow sticker."

"What's with the string?" Marvin asked.

"We are trying to stay one step ahead of the killer," Aristotle said. "Anticipating his next moves, trying to discern a pattern in these killings."

"And?" Marvin asked, looking at the unintelligible tangle of multicolored yarn.

"After much analysis of the relevant data, we have come to the conclusion that—there *is* no pattern. But"—and here he leaned in close to Marvin—"lack of a pattern *also* indicates something."

"Yes?" Marvin asked.

Aristotle leaned in even closer, whispering conspiratorially, "These killings are *random*."

"It does kind of look like a bird's nest," Ahab said.

"Yes, yes, we've *heard* your bird's-nest hypothesis before!" Aristotle shouted.

"Just tryin' to help, Aristotle," Ahab said, and slinked off.

"Let's continue with the tour," Aristotle said, turning back to Marvin. "Over here is our pantry." He indicated a stack of wool clothing. "Emergency rations, you know."

"Are those my sweaters?" Marvin asked, pulling one from the pile.

"Yes, I do believe we picked those up in here," Aristotle said. "But they're not a very good vintage. Rotten flavor. We shall definitely be eating those last."

He turned Marvin around and walked him over to a pile of assorted gadgets—kitchen utensils, small appliances, toys, exercise equipment. The moths must have dragged all the junk in from the neighboring attics. Marvin noticed that some of it had been strangely modified.

"Now we get to the real excitement," Aristotle said. "Our siege engines and field artillery."

He pointed to an exercise bike that, through a complicated assembly of springs, pulleys, ropes, and cookware, had been rigged to a broom handle attached to a colander. "This is my greatest creation," Aristotle said. "The eighteen-inch siege colander, with built-in straining capabilities. Best of all, by building it on a bicycle platform, I have made it extremely mobile."

"You know that's a stationary bike, don't you?" Marvin asked.

"Mobility is a state of mind," Aristotle said. "You do not understand the ancient art of war. *I* have studied." He handed Marvin an encyclopedia, which was open to an entry on catapults. "See? An exact replica!" Aristotle said.

Marvin looked at the illustration in the book and then at the moth's ramshackle creation. "Your catapult doesn't look anything like this," he said.

Aristotle snatched the book away. "I have *improved* upon the work of the ancients with modern technology," he said testily.

"Hey," Ahab interrupted. "Come and look at this."

He motioned them over to a corner of the room where the moths had stacked up five old television sets. Marvin saw that they had somehow tapped into the cable TV, and that each set was tuned to a different channel.

"Considering you were fleeing for your lives, you sure managed to bring a lot of stuff with you," Marvin said.

Suddenly, Sinclair Hackett, the mayor of Butcherville, flanked by the police commissioner, fire chief, and other local dignitaries, appeared on all five screens.

"Butcherville, this is our darkest hour. Right now." He glanced at his wristwatch. "Five o'clock. And it will get even darker, because daylight saving time ends in a few weeks. Just a reminder—your clocks need to be set back one hour. Much like our police department has been set back in their investigation of this relentless killer. Yes, they were asleep at the switch when our pets, our livestock, and our beloved *Big 'Un* . . ." Here the mayor paused, and everyone on the dais bowed their heads in memory of the elephant. ". . . were taken from us long before their time, by a foe too terrible to be withstood by our fat, lazy police force. Underskilled, overweight, and with no great store of intelligence . . . filled to the brim like vessels of raging incompetence—well, let's just say they blew it. But I promise you, one day, they *will* find this murderer, and bring him to justice." He slammed his fist on the podium for effect, his face turning slightly purple. "And then, the scattered remnant of our population that has survived the inevitable slaughter will rise up from the smoking ruins, band together, and rebuild this town brick by brick—with no compensation for their efforts, except for the memories of those who have gone before, and perhaps a brown-bag lunch. And, of course, they will vote for myself, your humble servant, in November's general election. Thank you. The police commissioner will now take your questions." The mayor dabbed his eyes with a handkerchief, and then ran off the stage.

The TV news stations cut away from the startled-looking police commissioner, who was being barraged with questions. An anchorman came onto the largest of the TVs the moths had collected, and nodded his head soberly. "Comforting words from our mayor during this dark time," he said. "And this just in—the Butcherville School Board is ready to make a special statement. We go live to Sam Fletcher, who is covering an emergency meeting at Butcherville High School. Sam?"

A field reporter appeared on-screen. "I'm here at Butcherville High, where the school board has been called into an emergency session to deal with the current crisis. The talk coming from school officials has been that they plan to suspend all classes at all schools until further notice."

Marvin's face lit up. "No school until further notice?" he said. "This is like my birthday, Christmas, and Halloween all rolled into one."

Sam Fletcher held his hand to his ear, listening to something over an earpiece. "I've just received word that school board president Smithsonia Welch is about to speak. Let's listen in."

The camera cut to a plump woman in glasses, who cleared her throat and looked down at her prepared notes. "In times of trouble such as these, I think back on my grandmother and her generation—the generation that built Butcherville. They were strong folk, filled with determination, gumption, and hardy whatnots. That spirit lives on today, especially in our children, who—we have decided—will not be cowed by this menace. My grandmother walked to school with only one foot, and would not have been stopped by elephants *or* vampires. If we forsake our children's education out of fear, then the Elephant Vampires of the world have *already* won. That is why, tomorrow morning, classes at all district schools will resume as scheduled. We call upon our children to commit these small acts of bravery, putting their own lives on the line to walk to school in defiance of the Elephant Vampire. Thank you."

Marvin's jaw dropped. He still wasn't convinced he was in any danger, but he was sure he'd rather spend a week at home reading comics than keep going to a building full of people who didn't like him very much.

"Well, guess that's it for you," Abraham said, drawing a claw across his throat in a cutting motion. "Walking to school defenseless. See you on the other side!"

"I did kind of prefer you guys on the other side," Marvin said. "You know, of the wall."

"Here," Ahab said, pulling a can of PLI Nonstick Pork Spray from his apron and handing it to Marvin.

"What's this?" Marvin asked.

"Your weapon," Ahab said. "To protect yourself on your suicidally dangerous walk to school."

"Stop saying that," Marvin said. He examined the list of ingredients on the can. "Wow," he said. "There actually is a lot of dangerous stuff in here." In the fine print, it said, "FOR COOKING ONLY; NOT FOR HUMAN CONSUMPTION."

"Yeah, you're going to need that," Abraham said. "You've got third watch tonight."

"What do you mean?" Marvin asked.

"We have set up a security perimeter and a four-shift Elephant Vampire Night-Watch rotation," Aristotle said. He gestured to a dry-erase board they had hung on the wall. It listed the sentry schedule. Abraham went over and erased a question mark that had been left as a placeholder in the "2 a.m. to 4 a.m." slot. He scribbled in *WEIRD KID*.

"I can't get up at two a.m.," Marvin said. "I have to go to school tomorrow. I need to sleep." He glanced around the room. He still hadn't really had time to digest what the moths had done to it yet. "Speaking of which, where's my bed?"

"It's a primary component of our barricade," Aristotle said. "Notice that the steel springs provide excellent repulsive capabilities. I'm thinking of filing a patent on this configuration." To Marvin, it all just looked like so much junk, piled haphazardly against the hole in the wall.

"Look," Marvin said. "I guess you guys can stay for now, but this is only temporary. I'm not going to have you occupying my room forever."

"This is not an occupation," Aristotle said. "We are here to liberate you!"

Abraham handed a mop and a bucket to Marvin. "And you can start by liberating those salad-dressing stains from the floor, recruit."

Marvin, still unsure how he had wound up at the bottom rank in his own bedroom, cleaned up the mess from the booby trap. It was after dark by the time he finished, and the multiple televisions made it impossible to concentrate on homework, so he decided to turn in early.

Marvin changed out of his oil-and-vinegar-soaked clothes and into pajamas. Then he gathered up some shirts and socks from his dresser (which had been propped against the wall as part of the barricade) and piled them up on the floor as his bed.

"Don't get too comfortable there," Abraham said as Marvin settled down to sleep on the lumpy, make-shift mattress. "I'm waking you up for sentry duty at oh-two-hundred sharp!"

The next morning, Marvin's alarm went off at 6:30 a.m. as usual. As he turned it off, he realized that no one had woken him for his watch shift. In one corner of the room, the three moths were slumped against one another, snoring loudly. Their improvised weapons had fallen from their hands. Marvin tucked a wire whisk back into Ahab's apron pocket and got ready for school.

11

The Smell of Victory

When Marvin returned to school, he realized, with delight, the true quality of the Elephant Vampire crisis. Everyone was too busy being scared of their own shadows to torment him. It was as if the whole town's pants had split on that gym rope, and now they were worried that their underwear was hanging out in the breeze. Marvin figured he owed the Elephant Vampire a debt of gratitude, whoever or whatever it was.

The one group of people the kids at school did make time to mock was the rest of Marvin's science class. Marvin and Fatima had been wearing protective gear that fateful day, but everyone else had been caught in the stink explosion, and now couldn't seem to wash away the odor. The smelly kids had been quarantined from the rest of the school and were being sequestered in a modular classroom outside the main building. Classes were being taught via videoconference, and the kids were subject to special arrival and departure procedures. Marvin watched one day as his smelly classmates were dropped off by their parents. He couldn't be sure, as the drop-off area was far from the main entrance, but it appeared that some of the parents—who were wearing largely ineffectual white paper surgical masks—actually shoved their kids out of the cars in their haste to be rid of them. Marvin heard one girl cry, "I love you, Mom! Don't forget to pick me up again this afternoon!" as her mother's car sped away with a sound of screeching tires.

One might blame the parents for that, except for the fact that the smelly kids were not able to stand their own smell. "You think you'd get used to it," a boy said to his similarly stinky classmate as they walked to the new classroom, "but you just don't!"

Even Little Stevie had been quarantined. He left his chauffeured car and walked proudly from the curb to the modular classroom, as the non-smelly students watched from behind a perimeter fence. Some of them started to taunt him, along with the other victims.

"Hey, moneybags! Couldn't afford a bath?"

"I always knew you were STINKIN' rich!"

"Hey! That walking pile of garbage looks just like Stevie!"

Stevie paused midstride, straightened his collar, and then turned around. His eyes were cold, cold with the threat of promised vengeance. He looked at all his detractors one by one, to let them know that he would remember the face of every person who had insulted him. Then he spoke.

"I may reek now," he said, "but that's just a temporary state. You will always be you. And I will ALWAYS be me. Never forget that." The students in the front of the crowd wilted visibly, then began to disperse, grumbling under their breath. Stevie turned and went into his classroom, whose door was marked with a makeshift sign that read ODORIFEROUS NEEDS.

At lunchtime, Marvin felt strangely liberated now that Stevie and his cohort were absent. He took his time going through the line, not worried that he might be teased or tripped or doused in shower-kraut. First, the Elephant Vampire scare had everyone too busy to think about what he was up to. And now, his chief tormentor was sidelined with a humiliating condition. Everything was coming up roses. And, Marvin thought to himself, roses did need a lot of fertilizer.

He paused as he passed by Stevie's table, which, while mostly empty, had attracted a crowd of "mourners." Stevie's hangers-on had erected an impromptu memorial to the missing. Photographs of Stevie and Amber stood at the head of the table, and they were surrounded by flowers and notes. A tray of food had been placed in front of Stevie's empty seat. The crowd of cronies held vigil with scented candles, comforting one another on their mutual loss.

"It's such a shame."

"Taken when they were so young and popular."

"And wealthy!"

"Yes. Very rich."

Marvin saw Fatima on the edge of the crowd, growing more and more perturbed. Finally, she blurted out, "But they're not dead!"

One of the kids nodded, and said, "Not as long as we remember them, and keep them in our hearts."

"No, I mean—"

Another groupie shushed her. "Have some respect!" she hissed at Fatima.

Fatima shook her head and turned away. She spotted Marvin and fell in step next to him as they walked through the cafetorium.

"I can see why no one has pieced this together," she said.

"Pieced what together?" Marvin said.

"But you never can be too careful," she continued, half to herself. She cast suspicious glances around the room. "Let's find somewhere private we can talk. Away from eavesdroppers."

"How about our lunch table?" Marvin said. "We're utterly alone there, if you recall."

They went to the table and sat down. They sat in silence for a minute, Fatima apparently lost in thought. "Pieced what together?" Marvin prompted.

"Hmm?" Fatima said, looking up. "Oh, yes. I mean our role in the incident. The authorities think it was a gas leak or some sort of stink bomb. Our classmates are too stupid to realize that our experiment on Lee was the cause. And the only adult present—"

"Miss Sweeney," Marvin said.

"—smells so bad that she's been asked to stay home on administrative leave."

"So it looks like we're off the hook!" Marvin said enthusiastically. "I have to say, this has been the *best* week."

"What?" Fatima said, horrified.

"Well, for me. No one's mentioned my underwear in days!"

"Big 'Un's a pile of bones, and you don't even care!" Fatima shouted. "You're a heartless doofus!"

Marvin held up his hands in a placating gesture. "That's not true! I care! I mean, I didn't know him personally, but I always threw him a peanut when I was at the zoo." Fatima just glared at him.

"Besides," he said, "I'm not even sure that the quote-unquote Elephant Vampire even exists."

"But, Big 'Un—" she started.

"We know he died," Marvin went on, "but nobody really knows how. And who's ever heard of an Elephant Vampire before? In fact, why are we even talking about vampires? News flash: I'm pretty sure vampires aren't real."

He took a forkful of food from his tray. "To be

honest, it all sounds too much like something from one of your crazy tabloids," Marvin said.

Fatima seethed quietly for a moment. Then she said, "To be honest, you *are* a little heartless." She stuck a finger in his face. "Look what you did to Lee."

"Me?" Marvin said. "You were there, too."

"I was there for the science," Fatima said. "And *I* feel sick about it. I can see why you don't have any friends."

"I did what I did in that science lab for you," Marvin said. "To shut up everyone who was making fun of you."

"Oh," she said. "Oh." She appeared to blush a little under all her headgear. "I thought it was just about Stevie. I . . . Thank you."

Marvin nodded, and they ate in silence for a moment.

Then Fatima looked up. "But I can't help feeling bad about Lee," she said, glancing over at his empty seat. "He's smellier than ever now, because of us, and he's trapped out there in quarantine. It's awful to be singled out like that."

"I guess I didn't think about what Lee's going through," Marvin said. "He must be miserable, stuck in that little room with Stevie and Amber and the rest of them."

"Have you tried reaching out to him at all?" Fatima said. "Maybe a phone call?"

"I don't know," Marvin said. "He was pretty mad at me after we walked him home that day."

"Well, maybe we'll see him at the assembly tomorrow," Fatima said. "You know, as much as I mistrust everything to do with Pork Loaf, I still can't believe that it had that big of an effect on Lee. What else is it capable of?"

The bell rang, and they both got up to clear their trays.

Walking home from school, Marvin found himself thinking more about Fatima's question. What else was Pork Loaf capable of? He had experimented with many of the raw ingredients over the years, and hadn't noticed anything strange, aside from the impossible-to-remove pork flavor. His last experiment had shown even less promise than usual—though that hadn't kept the moths from drinking it.

Marvin stopped in his tracks. The moths had drunk his experiment. The giant, superintelligent, mutant freeloaders inhabiting his room. A terrible realization began growing in his mind, and Marvin ran the rest of the way home.

When Marvin entered his attic room, the moths were eating a late lunch of upholstery—apparently an old sofa cushion they had brought from one of the other attics.

"You can't have any," Abraham said through a full mouth. "We only packed enough emergency rations for three."

"So, you just eat whatever you find up here?" Marvin asked. "You eat or drink whatever's lying around?"

"Well we are not *cannibals,* if that's what you mean," Aristotle said.

"No, that's not what I meant," Marvin said.

"Then get to it, boy," Abraham said between slurps. "Time's a-wasting."

"Did you drink my experiment?" Marvin asked, looking from one giant insect to another.

"What are you talking about?" Abraham said. "What experiment?"

"The test tubes of Pork Punch," Marvin said. "I left them here, and I seem to recall that they were on your coffee table when I first met you."

"Oh," Abraham said. "Yeah, probably. This old wool gets a little dry, you know."

Marvin turned to Aristotle, who he knew to be the most scientifically minded of the three. "I think that's what made you what you are."

"An intriguing hypothesis," said Aristotle. "And also one that's conveniently impossible to verify."

"Well, how do you think you three became different from all the other moths up here in the attic?" Marvin asked.

"Good jeans?" Ahab said uncertainly, a pair of designer denim jeans hanging out of his mandibles.

"That's *genes* as in DNA, not Jordache, you hulking nincompoop," Aristotle said. "And those are cotton, by the way." Ahab spit the pants ungloriously onto the floor, where they landed with a soggy plop.

"Look," Marvin said, frustrated, "*that* is a normal moth." He pointed to a tiny insect, no bigger than his fingernail, that fluttered out of the air and settled onto the pile of wool in front of Abraham.

"Hey!" Abraham shouted, shooing the tiny moth away. "Off my lunch, cretin!" He crushed it against a nearby beam. "Never did like that guy," he muttered.

"I thought you said you weren't cannibals," Marvin said, horrified.

"Well I'm not going to *eat* him," Abraham replied. "What's your point, anyway?"

"That my experiment—a strange mixture of ingredients from PLI's labs—had an unexpected effect upon you three," Marvin said, his eyes unfocused. "It mutated you, causing you to grow hundreds of times larger and achieve incredible levels of intelligence. In short, *I am your creator.*"

"And if I could consistently hit home runs out of Fenway, I'd be Ted Williams," said Abraham. "But wishing it don't make it so."

Aristotle, meanwhile, was nodding to himself. "No, let us consider. It *would* explain our rapid transformation immediately following the ingestion of the colorful liquid," he said. "Liquid that was unlabeled and unmarked, I might add. Not that we could read at that point. Nevertheless"—and he pointed a long appendage at Marvin in an accusatory manner—"sloppy science, my dear Watson."

Ahab suddenly leaped to his feet. "Daddy!" he cried, then ran forward and engulfed Marvin in a crushing four-armed hug.

"So what are the implications of this, I wonder?" Aristotle said.

"For starters, he can't complain about us staying here anymore," Abraham said. "*If* he wants to be a responsible parent, that is. Right, Pops?"

"Great," Marvin said from within Ahab's furry embrace. "Welcome home, kids."

12

The Swine in Pearls Brigade

Marvin stood in a line of kids at school, waiting to get into the cafetorium for a special assembly. He heard a clanking approaching him from behind, accompanied by disgruntled mutterings and exclamations.

"Hey, watch it!"

"That's my spot in line! No cutting!"

"Out of the way! Public Safety! Public Safety!" The last voice was clearly Fatima's, and Marvin hoped that if he stood completely still, the back of his head would blend in with all the other nondescript heads behind him, and she would be unable to find him to invoke whatever public-safety protocol she was shouting about.

"Marvin! There you are," she said at last, and Marvin sighed. "I've got important news."

"What's the public-safety emergency?" he asked.

"What? Oh that's just my thing," she said.

"It is?"

"Yeah—if I want people to get out of my way, I yell, 'Public Safety,'" she said. "It's more effective than 'Excuse me.' I've tested it."

"Great. I'm sorry I asked," Marvin said.

"It's about the moths," she said, her voice suddenly dropping to a whisper.

"That reminds me," Marvin said. "I have some big news about the moths, too."

"Are you thinking what I'm thinking?" she asked. "Let's both say it at the same time. Ready? One, two, three!"

"I made the moths," Marvin blurted.

"The moths are the killers!" Fatima said gleefully.

"I—what?" Marvin said.

"Yes! I think THEY are actually the Elephant Vampire," she said. "I was looking back over the timeline of the killings—"

"That's how you spend your free time?" Marvin interrupted.

She ignored him and barreled on. "And your discovery of the moths exactly matches up with the first animal disappearances. Plus, just think about it—who else would be strong enough to take down an elephant like Big 'Un? Maybe GIANT INSECTS?" She finally paused and thought about what Marvin had said. "You made the moths. You made the moths what?"

"I made the moths . . . clean up after themselves," Marvin said, grinning lamely.

"*That's* your big news?" she said. "I don't think you understand the concept of 'big news.'"

"Let's call it 'highly unexpected news,'" he said.

"Let's not."

"Can we at least agree that they'd be unlikely to do that?" he said.

"I suppose so," Fatima said. "Because I'd expect them to be, oh, I don't know, *sucking the life from their next victims!*"

"They can't be the killers," Marvin said. "They're just big dopes who like to eat wool and watch baseball."

"They're mutants!" she said. "Who knows what they're capable of? Or where they even came from? Whoever created them must have had a sick agenda and a dark, twisted mind."

"Or, maybe," Marvin said, swallowing nervously, "he was just having a bad day. And even though this researcher—let's call him 'Martin'—was trying to do science responsibly, he accidentally mixed some stuff together, and left it lying around for a few days, unattended, and maybe some normal moths just happened to drink it—"

He looked up and saw that Fatima was glaring at him. Her arms were stiff at her sides, and she was angrily drumming the fingers of one hand against her knee brace. *Clackety-clack. Clackety-clack.*

"It's just a theory," Marvin said.

"You idiot," she said. "You did some dumb, reckless experiment and created those giant moths, didn't you?"

"One person's 'dumb and reckless' is another person's 'pioneering and innovative,'" Marvin said. "Just ask Alexander Fleming about his moldy bread."

"Fleming's discovery of penicillin saved millions of people," she shot back. "*Your* creations are draining the lifeblood of pachyderms and countless stray cats."

"Okay, so maybe they're not *exactly* the same . . ." Marvin said.

"You admit it then?" Fatima said. "You admit that you created those monsters?"

"Look, I wasn't setting out to create giant insects," he said. "Just better-tasting Pork Punch. So I mixed together some of the raw ingredients to find the perfect blend. And this wasn't it—let me tell you. I took one swig and spit the whole thing right back into the container. Then I guess some ordinary moths drank it, and—well, the results are living in my bedroom."

"Your clean bedroom?" she asked.

"No, that part was—well, not exactly true," Marvin admitted. "Call it wishful thinking."

"So let me get this straight," Fatima said, folding her arms. "You took a product that we know has dire effects on living specimens—like Lee—and introduced human DNA to it?"

"What?"

"When you took a mouthful and spat it back in, your saliva entered the mix," she said. "Now human DNA—your DNA—has been combined with whatever noxious chemicals are already present in Pork Loaf products."

"I didn't think of that," Marvin admitted.

"Big surprise," she said. "You know, this all makes perfect sense now. Not only do those moths have your DNA, they have your infuriating personality traits, too."

"My personality traits?"

"Yes! Abraham—that's the little round one, right?—he has your sarcasm and rudeness. And Aristotle is like a reflection of your intellectual side," she said. "Honestly, I thought he would be shorter, given the source material."

"Hey!" Marvin said. "Well, don't forget about Ahab. He's just a big sweetheart. Who couldn't love him?"

"Maybe his victims," Fatima said. "You know, as they were having their fluids sucked through his long proboscis?"

Up ahead, the line finally started moving. "Take your seats, please," a teacher called out to the students. Marvin and Fatima walked along with the crowd.

"You're wrong about the moths," Marvin said. "They wouldn't hurt a fly. I mean, they did ambush me and beat me with kitchen utensils once, but that was a misunderstanding."

"Believe what you want," Fatima said. "I know *I* wouldn't be able to sleep in that room with those murderers. And I definitely wouldn't be able to sleep knowing that *I* was the one who created them."

Marvin shuffled into the cafetorium with the rest of the students, trying to ignore her warning. He couldn't believe that the moths were capable of such horrific acts.

But he also couldn't quite get the idea out of his mind.

As Marvin walked into the cafetorium, he saw the cheery banner of the Swine in Pearls Theater Brigade. The community acting troupe had visited Marvin's elementary school each year, performing instructional dramas like *Good Neighbors Don't Cut in Line*, *Raise Your Hand if You've Got to Go*, and Marvin's personal favorite, *You Can Pick Your Friends, but You Can't Pick Your Friend's Nose*. Representatives from the police and fire departments stood at the side of the room.

Marvin also noticed that the Odoriferous Needs students had been brought in from their modular classroom and were seated in a roped-off area to one side of the room. The fire exits stood open, and large fans positioned in front of them were sucking the unpleasant stench out of the building.

In the middle of the cordoned-off crowd of students, Lee was holding court, dispensing wisdom to the newly smelly. Marvin was surprised at just how confident—even happy—Lee appeared to be.

"What about those commercial skunk-spray removers?" one boy asked Lee.

Lee shook his head. "Those don't work as well as you think," he said. "Lots of hype. Best to stick to the basics. Baking soda baths are good. And wear natural fibers—they breathe better."

The girl to Lee's left, Olivia Muntz, looked uncomfortable as she struggled with how to phrase her question. "But do you really want the—odor—to get out?" she said. "Wouldn't it be better to trap it in?"

"No," Lee said. "Ventilation is your friend. The last thing you want is a buildup." The other children nodded solemnly. "Make sure you always leave the bedroom window cracked, just a little, when you go to sleep," he added, looking at his audience one by one. "Or else, when you wake up in the morning, you might pass out again from the concentrated smell."

"That happened to me this morning!" a boy said. "My dad used a pair of barbecue tongs to drag me out of my room."

"Been there," Lee said. "One time, I missed school for a week because of that. My grandmother thought I had the flu."

Fatima watched Lee, a look of surprise on her face. "He looks great," she said to Marvin as they walked to the front of the room. "He really seems to be coming into his own."

Lee glanced over at Marvin as they passed. Marvin gave a small wave, but Lee turned back to his listeners without any sign of recognition. Marvin saw Stevie and Amber sitting toward the edge of the smelly crowd, clearly not happy with their place in the world. They ignored Lee and talked quietly to each other.

Fatima and Marvin sat near the front, close to the stage that took up one wall. Once the crowd filled in, recorded music began to play, signaling the start of the show. The troupe's players marched out on stage, dressed in black pants and turtlenecks and white gloves.

They skulked around the front of the room, doing an interpretive "Vampire Dance," before finally breaking into song:

> Stop, drop, and roll.
> Stop, drop, and roll.
> Protect your neck;
> Protect your soul.
> Stop, drop, and roll.
> Stop, drop, and roll.
> Don't let him put
> You into a hole!

They danced around some more, actors alternately playing the parts of the Elephant Vampire or his victims, some of whom panicked and were "killed," while others confidently followed the song's instructions and rolled away to safety. They sang a few more verses before belting out the final chorus:

> If you see the Elephant Vampire, what do you do?
> Stop, drop, and roll—that'll save you!

Stop, drop, and roll—
THAT . . . WILL . . . SAAA-AAAVE . . .
YOUUUUUUU!!!

The troupe's leader stepped forward. "Remember, kids," she said, "only you can prevent Elephant Vampires!" All the actors bowed.

Everyone applauded, and then a police officer stepped in front of the actors and said, "Great job. Just great. Now, are there any questions?"

Several hands shot up. The officer pointed to the first student. The kid stood up and said, "My uncle Jim is an actor, and my mom says he's a bum."

The police officer looked to the troupe leader. "Do you want to take this one?"

She stepped forward. "Most actors I know are very kind and dedicated to their craft."

Someone else asked the police officer, "Can you see in the dark?"

"No," said the officer.

"Then how are you going to catch the Elephant Vampire?"

The officer rolled his eyes. "What I meant to say

was, Officer Smith here can see in the dark," he said, motioning to his partner.

The auditorium erupted into cheers.

"Can he fly?"

"Yes, Officer Smith can fly, too," he said curtly. More cheers.

"Can we see him fly?"

"Next question," the officer said.

"I have a question," Fatima said, standing up. "How in the world will stopping, dropping, and rolling protect us from a killer—or *killers*"—she squinted sideways at Marvin—"that could take down a six-ton bull elephant?"

"Let me answer your question by asking you another question," the officer said. "Do you think that this big, stumpy-legged elephant could stop, drop, and roll?"

Fatima thought about it a moment. "No, probably not," she said.

"Well, there you have it," the officer said.

One of the actors stepped forward. "It's very difficult for a vampire to bite your neck if you're rolling on the ground," he said. "Believe me, we tried it."

"Plus, if you're on fire, it will put the flames out," said the assistant fire chief.

"Why would I be on fire?" Fatima asked.

The fire chief shrugged. "You'd be surprised how often it happens to me."

Marvin raised his hand. "How do we know the Elephant Vampire is even real?" he asked. "I mean, no one's even seen him."

The police officer frowned. "Well, then how do *you* explain what happened to Big 'Un?"

"I don't know," Marvin said, "but just because an elephant died doesn't mean an Elephant Vampire killed him. I mean, an Elephant Vampire sounds like something out of one of those crazy tabloids with stories about UFOs and bigfoot." Fatima shot Marvin a dirty look. "It could be some sort of spontaneous dehydration problem. Animals are mostly water, you know, and those elephants *do* eat a lot of peanuts."

"I say we listen to him," a voice called out from the back of the room. Marvin turned and saw that it was his cousin, Stevie. "After all, if anyone knows how to communicate with elephants, it's Tarzan!"

The students—stinky and fresh-smelling alike—

erupted into laughter. Stevie gave Marvin a knowing look that told his cousin he wasn't out of the game yet.

The principal, Evander "E-Man" Calypso, stepped out in front of the crowd, waving his hands for quiet. He was a big man, a former linebacker who had gone into education after he retired from professional football. "Okay, everyone," he said. "The E-Man thinks we should give a big round of applause to all of our performers and first responders." Everyone clapped enthusiastically. "Now, the E-Man knows you all want to do your part to help catch the Elephant Vampire, but the school board, mayor, and police commissioner have decided it would be best if everyone stayed indoors and out of the way. Therefore, we're canceling *all* Harvest Festival activities next weekend, including the bonfire, the parade, the fair, and the school dance."

The applause died, quickly replaced with shouts of dismay from the students. All except for Marvin.

"Oh, thank goodness," Marvin said. Fatima scowled but said nothing.

In the Odoriferous Needs section, Amber Bluestone got to her feet. "You can't cancel the dance," she shouted. "I have to be queen!"

"Queen of what?" someone shouted. "Queen of the landfill?" A few chuckles broke out in response.

Stevie stood and stared directly at the principal. "I have the best minds on three continents flying in to treat my . . . condition," Stevie said. "A perfumer from Paris, a chemical-warfare expert, and a Nobel-winning zoologist who is *the* authority on skunks. I *will* be ready for the dance, and I *will* claim my crown."

The principal calmly shook his head. "The E-Man is sorry, but the decision is final, and—"

Little Stevie pointed an angry finger at the principal. "I'll have your job, you hack!"

The E-Man, though he stood over six feet tall, shrank somewhat in the face of Stevie's anger. He stuttered out, "The, uh, the E-Man understands you might be disappointed. But the E-Man thought that, instead of singing songs at a bonfire, watching a parade, eating cotton candy, and going out dancing with your friends, maybe you might enjoy staying inside and reading these *free safety comics!*" The principal reached into a cardboard box behind him and threw handfuls of comic books into the crowd. The children reacted with excitement, until they saw the titles.

The children grumbled their general discontent. "This . . . this is a travesty," Marvin said, staring at the Fearless Phil comic book in his hands. He couldn't believe that his hero had been reduced to telling stupid children not to stick forks into electrical outlets.

"What do any of these comic books have to do with the current crisis?" Fatima asked, waving a copy of Cautious Kitty.

"A little caution never hurt anyone," the police officer said. "Wouldn't you agree?"

She furrowed her brow. "Well, yes, but—"

"That's enough questions for today," said the E-Man. The assistant fire chief waved to him, and the principal nodded and winked. "And one final announcement from the fire department before you're dismissed."

The assistant fire chief stepped forward, taking his hat off and running a hand over his close-shaved gray hair. "Kids, I'm gonna talk straight to you," he said. "Once you're past the age of seven, there's no more time for foolin' around. I know a bunch of you out there think you're pretty funny. Well guess what? We don't have time for pranksters and jokers. That's why, after the other day's little *stunt* in the science lab, we refurbished all the fire alarms in this building with an explosive dye pack. I want you to know that your actions have consequences. You pull one of those fire alarms, you're gettin' a face full of blue. You WILL be caught. And we WILL come down on you. Hard. Think you can hide from me? That blue dye *never* washes off. I'll see your blue face at school, at the mall, when you're eating your pizza pie!"

One of the kids called out, "But what if there's an actual fire?"

The fireman whirled on him. "I said we don't have time for pranksters, and we don't have time for smart alecks, either!"

"That will be all," the principal said. "Dismissed."

Marvin turned to Fatima. "Huh," he said, standing up to leave. "Explosive dye packs?"

Fatima dismissed it with a wave of her hand. "Pfft. That's nonsense. Didn't you see that wink from the principal? They're just spreading some urban legend so that everyone will be too afraid to pull the fire alarms."

"At least the Harvest Dance is canceled," Marvin said. "Now we don't have to go through that whole charade."

"Yes, I'm sure you're glad you don't have to go to the dance with me," Fatima said, her face dark.

Marvin stared at her for a moment. "Now that I think about it," he said, "if there's no dance that night . . ." He trailed off and raised an expectant eyebrow at her.

"Yes, Marvin?" Fatima asked, excited.

"Do you think I can get my money back on the tickets?"

Fatima huffed in frustration and stormed out of the cafetorium, leaving Marvin alone with his thoughts.

He was somewhat frustrated that she hadn't answered his question.

13

The Letter *V*

Two weeks had passed since the death of Big 'Un, and the level of tension in the town was growing greater every day. The authorities still had no leads on the whereabouts of the Elephant Vampire, and public outrage over city hall's ineffective leadership was nearing the breaking point.

At home, Marvin was trying to make the best of life with his new roommates. He was not used to such close quarters, particularly when the roommates were so large, hairy, and inhuman. Also, they never stopped watching the round-the-clock TV news coverage about the Elephant Vampire situation, which made it hard for Marvin to concentrate on his homework.

At every hour of the day, the stations had breaking news reports about the Elephant Vampire panic; most had discontinued all regular programming. Channel 7 began each ten-minute news block with an animated title that swooshed on-screen. A scary vampire head appeared, the mouth opening wide to reveal oversize fangs. Then, the camera zoomed in tight on the upper fangs, which morphed into large letter *Vs*. Finally, the full title appeared: "CRISIS: VAMPIRE VATCH IN THE 'VILLE," backed by Stars and Stripes graphics in red, white, and blue.

"Velcome to Vampire Vatch," said the anchor, with obvious distaste. He paused, then looked off camera. "Do I really have to say this every time, Larry?" Viewers couldn't hear Larry's reply, but the anchor eventually went back to reading his script, though without much enthusiasm. What followed were endless segments on the police department's hunt for the Elephant Vampire. They showed clips of embedded reporters who followed members of the SWAT team as they battered down the doors of mausoleums around town, seeking out the vampire's hiding place. Forensic investigators ran tests on Big 'Un's empty carcass to find any clue to the vampire's identity and methods. There was also a story about a copycat vampire: The man had been frightening local residents, until they realized that he was just wearing plastic Halloween fangs. After that, they beat him with rakes and locked him in a shed until the authorities arrived.

Marvin just shook his head. "This is ridiculous," he said.

Abraham nodded. "Yeah, completely ridiculous. Where's the National Guard?"

"That's not what I meant—" Marvin said, but Ahab shushed him.

"The weather's up next!" he said.

The weather report indicated clear skies for the next week: "Perfect vampire-tracking weather," the meteorologist said, smiling.

Despite the sunny skies and the police department's many efforts, it was obvious that no significant progress was being made in the investigation. The experts began weighing in on the continuing danger posed by the apparently untraceable Elephant Vampire. Channel 5 ran a "point/counterpoint" program with two pundits who stood on opposite sides of the debate over how dangerous the Elephant Vampire really was.

"POINT: This Elephant Vampire has proved to be impossible to see, impossible to track, and wholly bereft of the milk of human kindness. It is my scientific conclusion that the Elephant Vampire is going to kill us all."

"COUNTERPOINT: I disagree. Let's keep a level head here. I think that only *most* of us will die at the hands of the Elephant Vampire. A good forty percent of us may survive with some slight to severe mangling. Of that forty percent, half will likely be turned into Elephant Vampires themselves, and feed upon the remainder. So the Elephant Vampire *itself* will hardly kill us *all*."

The public television station ran an interview with a spokesperson from PorkPeace. "We should not be so quick to condemn the Elephant Vampire," he said. "After all, our industrialized society is responsible for destroying its natural habitat, thereby driving it into our town in search of food. Considering the ongoing decline of the worldwide elephant population, we can only surmise that the Elephant Vampire, too, is on the brink of extinction. Rather than killing this misunderstood creature, as so many in our government are only too eager to do, we should instead capture and tag it, so that we can conduct further study. Who knows?

Many plants and animals produce unique compounds that have proved invaluable to medical science. Would we hunt to extinction a being that might hold the secret to curing cancer, tooth decay, or halitosis? Given these facts, PorkPeace is introducing a bill into the state legislature that would declare the entire town of Butcherville to be a protected habitat for the Elephant Vampire, and make any hunting of this majestic, but vanishing, beast illegal."

There was even a lifestyle piece on one of the cable gossip networks. Entitled "IN or OUT?" it advised viewers on the latest up-to-the-minute trends in the world of fashion, food, and home decorating during what they had enthusiastically dubbed "Vampire Week."

FASHION:
OUT: plunging necklines, dark colors
IN: turtleneck sweaters, puncture-resistant fabric

TABLETOP:
OUT: blood oranges, plastic forks
IN: roasted garlic, sterling silver knives

HOME DECORATING:
OUT: open windows, fresh air
IN: wrought iron bars, mirrors

All of it was driving the moths to new heights of paranoia. They installed additional locks on the door and on all the windows. In a fit of panic, they had even put locks on the drawers of Marvin's dresser, which severely limited his fashion choices. The moths had taken to planning for a number of absurd survival scenarios, rehearsing each one in turn, with one of them acting the part of the Elephant Vampire. Only once did they try to enlist Marvin's help.

"All right," Abraham said, draping a dusty plastic cape from some forgotten Halloween costume over Marvin's shoulders. "We're not sure if the Elephant Vampire has the ability to transform himself or not, but we should be prepared for any eventuality. In this attack scenario, he turns himself into fog and comes up through the steam pipes, rematerializing in solid form right here." He indicated an area of the floor with two of his arms. "The countermeasure is this cinder block, which we will drop on top of his skull." Off to the side, Ahab hefted a large concrete block.

"I need you to play the Elephant Vampire," Abraham continued. "Stand here, and pretend to be fog. Then, when you're fully rematerialized, give us a signal, and Ahab here will brain you. Okay?" Ahab practiced lifting the block over his head and swinging it straight down again.

"Yeah, I think I'll pass," Marvin said, untying the cape. "I have algebra homework, and I don't think I can do it without my brains inside my skull."

"Fine," Abraham said huffily, snatching the cape back. "Baby. But don't come crying to me when the Elephant Vampire rematerializes inside your locker and you don't know what to do."

At school, the kids were mostly upset about the rigid curfew and the cancellation of the Harvest Festival and Dance—except Marvin. That Friday, Marvin sat in the school library with Fatima during seventh-period study hall, looking forward to a weekend of binge-reading Fearless Phil comics instead of enduring the inevitable embarrassment of the Harvest Dance. He reached into his backpack and pulled out a notebook, along with the latest issue of Fearless Phil, which he laid out on the library table.

"Can I take a look at your notes from science class?" he asked her. "Mine got a little scorched during the experiment." Their science classes had finally resumed, but not in the lab, whose door had been sealed with airtight plastic sheeting and covered with DO NOT ENTER signs. At first, the school administrators had been concerned that small animals would get in through the broken windows, but none had shown any interest. Marvin and Fatima's class was meeting in the home economics kitchen, which at least allowed them to use sinks and stovetop burners. There had been a confused moment, however, when the dissection instructions and the braised frog legs recipes had gotten mixed up.

"Here," Fatima said, sliding her bag across the table to him. "They're in the black binder."

Marvin opened the bag, which contained eight identical black three-ring binders. He pulled one out at random and opened it. It was not filled with class notes. In fact, it wasn't filled with notes at all, but rather pictures of women's dresses cut out of fashion magazines, fabric swatches, pressed flowers, photos of men's suits, and pages torn out of *Soap Opera Secrets Weekly*, with various plot points highlighted and diagrammed.

Marvin flipped deeper into the binder, and was stunned to see several pages of photos—of himself. They had apparently been taken when he wasn't looking; there were shots of him eating lunch, nodding off in class, and picking his ear. They were tagged with notes like, *CON: Talks with mouth full, PRO: Cute face, CON: No butt, PRO: Tucks in shirt, PRO: Good listener,* and *CON: Makes rude comments about what he just listened to me say.*

Then Marvin came across a manila envelope that had been slid in among the pages. On the front it was stamped CONFIDENTIAL: MY EYES ONLY. Marvin slipped the contents out and began reading.

EVALUATION AND PROPOSED ADVANCEMENT OF QUALITY BOYFRIEND CHARACTERISTICS IN PREEXISTING SIXTH-GRADE SUBJECT

HYPOTHESIS: Marvin could be a good boyfriend if the following improvements were made:

i. Hardier exercise regimen. Subject lacks upper-body strength, as evidenced by performance in "Tarzan" incident.

ii. Dietary and lifestyle changes. Subject appears pale and underrested. Recommend eight hours uninterrupted sleep each night, better nutrition, and more time spent outside of dark attic.

iii. Etiquette training. Subject has adequate personal grooming habits, but is utterly lacking in social niceties. Recommend intense two-day "Sgt. Manners" boot camp.

iv. Motivational training. Subject has no drive or ambition, aside from desire to be left alone. Recommend seminar with renowned motivational speaker Stryker Horsefeed on "Embracing Your Inner Genghis Khan."

Marvin quietly closed the binder and tried to slide it back into the bag, but a swatch of pale-blue silk fluttered out of the pages and drifted onto the table in front of Fatima. She looked up at him in alarm and rage.

"Not *that* one!" she shouted, snatching the entire bag back from him. "Who told you you could open *that* one?"

"They—are—all . . . looking the same?" Marvin stuttered. "Why can't you be like a normal girl and just draw hearts all over it? Then I'd know not to open it."

"It's typical of you to add indecency to humiliation," Fatima said.

"What are you talking about?" Marvin said.

"It wasn't enough for you to make Lee smelly, you had to push it all the way and make him untouchable," she said.

"Hold on a minute—" Marvin said.

"As for me, I'm already an untouchable, apparently," she said. "I mean, it's bad enough you never wanted to go to the dance with me, but now you're invading my secret thoughts."

"To be fair, your secrets weren't all that secure," Marvin said. "Not even well labeled, really."

"How dare you!" Fatima said, insulted that her organizational skills would be impugned. "Well, it doesn't matter now," she said. "The dance has been canceled. Fifty hours of research out the window."

"Fifty hours of research?" Marvin said. "On what?"

"On the dance!" Fatima said. She slapped the binder. "This is my complete plan of action for the Harvest Dance—what to wear, how to behave, what to do when you come to pick me up, what to do if you"—she looked at the floor and blushed deeply—"kiss me at the end of the night . . ."

Marvin stared at her, dumbfounded. At that moment, he realized that the passage of time was all a matter of perception. He looked up at the library clock and saw that the hands were no longer moving. The idea that Fatima could consider him to be boyfriend material—it was harder for Marvin to grasp than the notion of giant moths or Elephant Vampires that liquefied and devoured their prey. At least those things had a basis in reality. That long moment of reflection and discomfort—and reflection on the discomfort—seemed to stretch out for an eternity. But then the library doors burst open, and time swung back into full speed.

Charging through the doors came Little Stevie's

mom, Constance Upton, flanked by a half dozen police officers. She clapped her hands for attention. "Children, remain where you are," she said. "This won't take long." She turned to a police officer. "Lieutenant, do your duty."

The officer nodded, and he and his men fanned out and began pulling books from the library shelves. Mrs. Goudy, the librarian, strode out from behind her desk. "What's the meaning of this?" she asked Mrs. Upton. The two women stood glaring at each other, nose to nose, Marvin's aunt in her impeccably tailored pantsuit, rectangular designer glasses, and carefully coiffed auburn hair, and the librarian in a long cotton skirt with a floral print, sandals, and long, roughly braided graying hair.

"Hello, Chrissy," Constance said.

"It's Chrysanthemum to you, fascist," Mrs. Goudy replied. "Why are your goons ransacking my library?"

"They're protecting the children," Mrs. Upton said, a triumphant smile creeping onto her lips.

"Against what—knowledge?"

Mrs. Upton looked at her nemesis through narrowed eyes. "Not all knowledge is good," she said.

"And not all *keepers* of knowledge are good." Constance pulled a sheet of paper from her designer purse. "I've been specially authorized by the school board to provide guidance and leadership in protecting our children's tender young minds from the corrupting influence of the Elephant Vampire's radical ideology. As such, we're confiscating any books deemed harmful to the student body." She handed the sheet to the librarian. "If you would be so kind as to assist the officers in finding any of the volumes on this list, I'm sure the authorities would greatly appreciate it."

Mrs. Goudy tore the sheet of paper into tiny pieces, which she let flutter to the floor. She folded her arms and stared at Constance.

Any trace of a smile left Mrs. Upton's face. "Very well, Chrysanthemum. Your insubordination will be remembered."

The police officers began filling up wheelbarrows with armloads of books. They started with "occult" titles, such as Bram Stoker's *Dracula* and Mary Shelley's *Frankenstein*. Next came wildlife books on elephants. They pulled the *E* and *V* volumes of the encyclopedia off the shelf and ripped pages out of dictionaries.

"To be safe, your men should take any title that starts with an *E* or a *V*," Mrs. Upton instructed the lieutenant.

The look on Fatima's face grew increasingly angry. Finally, she asked Mrs. Upton, "Why are you taking the whole *V* section? If you're worried about vampires, just remove the vampire books and leave the rest."

Constance turned to her. "That *V* has been a menace to our town for decades—vampires, voodoo, Vlad the Impaler, aka Dracula, veganism . . . I'm just making sure that it can no longer be a threat to our values—I mean, morals."

The lieutenant stared at the shelves for a long time. "Uhhh . . ." he said, "the books aren't organized alphabetically."

"What do you mean?" Mrs. Upton snapped.

A wide grin spread across Mrs. Goudy's face. "Dewey decimals, Constance."

"That's another thing that will have to change," Mrs. Upton said. "No more hiding your filth with the help of some arcane filing system." She paused and considered the situation for a moment. "Lieutenant," she said at last, "you can send your men back next week to go through the rest of the *Es* and *Vs*. We have enough here for the event tonight. Don't forget the posters."

He nodded and signaled two of his men. They went out, then came back with rolled-up posters and an old-fashioned push broom and a bucket of paste, the kind used to hang billboards. They slapped the posters up on the windows and even over a wall mural that had been painted by the students. The mural showed a boy and a girl happily reading, with a large thought balloon coming out of their heads, filled with characters from literature. *Books open your mind,* it read. A few seconds later, the mural was covered in several places by large black posters with red letters that said:

BUTCHERVILLE UNITED

Rally, bonfire, book-burning, and weenie roast

today at 5 p.m.

Memorial Park

Sponsored by the Pork Loaf

Ladies' Auxiliary

"Freedom is burning bright!"

Constance nodded in approval, then turned to the students with a smile. "Good news, children. The Harvest Festival Bonfire is back on. As an added bonus, we'll be celebrating this important moment in your young lives by turning the false and harmful ideas that undermine our common good into ash," she announced. "Dress appropriately!"

"I'll be there," Mrs. Goudy said. "PorkPeace will be there to protest this injustice."

"Don't forget to bring some marshmallows," Constance said, turning to leave. On her way out, she snatched Marvin's Fearless Phil comic book from the table.

"Hey!" Marvin said.

"Comic books make children stupid," Constance said sharply.

"Then why did the school board give us all free safety comics at the assembly?" Marvin asked.

Constance simply snorted through her nose and stormed out the door without further explanation.

"I can't believe this," Fatima said to Marvin. "How can someone be holding a book-burning in this day and age? We're just giving in to the worst elements of mob mentality." She looked to Marvin for a reply. "Are you even listening to me?"

Marvin glanced up. "Sorry—I'm still in shock." He looked at the empty place on the table in front of him. "Apparently, the comics made me stupid." He then looked over and saw Fatima's Harvest Dance binder poking out of her bag. "And seeing the contents of your kissy-face binder didn't help, either."

Fatima scowled and picked up the offending notebook. She walked across the room and flung it into a wheelbarrow full of books destined for the rally as one of the officers pushed it out the door.

"There!" she said to Marvin. "Happy now?"

"I don't see how anyone could be happy at a time like this," he said.

"That's more like it," Fatima said.

"I mean, you can destroy the binder, but you can't destroy my memories," Marvin said.

Fatima frowned. "We're talking about the book-burning!" she said.

"Right. Of course," Marvin said. "The rally." He thought quietly for a moment, his brow furrowing. "Hey," he said. "If the Elephant Vampire is still allegedly on the loose, isn't it a little dangerous to be holding it so close to sunset?"

"I hadn't thought about that," she said. "I was too busy being outraged to think about the danger."

"Well, maybe there is no Elephant Vampire, and the only thing you have to worry about is living in a police state," he said.

"Or maybe there *is* an Elephant Vampire, and he's living in your attic," she said.

"That's *probably* not true," Marvin said uneasily. "I hope." The class bell rang, and they gathered up their things and left.

Memorial Park was filled with people by the time Marvin and his family arrived. A large circle had been cleared for the bonfire itself, which was piled high with books and lumber, waiting to be lit. Marvin passed a mom and dad and their small children, who were clinging to their parents' legs.

"Dad, I want to go home," the little boy said. "I don't want to be eaten by the Elephant Vampire."

"Don't worry," the father said, patting his son on

the head. "I'm sure the authorities wouldn't have us here if it wasn't safe."

The next couple Marvin passed didn't have as much faith in the powers that be. "It's been more than two weeks already," the man said to his wife. "When are they going to *do* something?"

As Marvin and his family continued to move up through the crowd for a better view, they heard the sound of chanting and shouting. A dozen members of PorkPeace, including the librarian Mrs. Goudy, were waving protest signs that read, LEARNING, NOT BURNING, A BOOK A DAY KEEPS IGNORANCE AWAY, and EDUCATION, NOT RETALIATION. A wall of police officers was keeping the rest of the people—some of whom were growing increasingly angry—away from the activists.

"Get lost, vampire lovers!" someone shouted at the protesters.

"Free thought isn't free!" screamed another person.

"You're putting us in the poorhouse with your overdue book fees, Goudy!"

Marvin's mom shook her head at the high

emotions, and especially at the large red Pork Loaf Ladies' Auxiliary banner up on the main stage.

"I don't understand it," she said. "Why is the PLLA sponsoring a book-burning? I never would have allowed such a thing when I was president. I need to speak to Constance."

Marvin watched his neighbors pile on fuel for the bonfire. In addition to the books the police had removed from school and public libraries, townspeople had brought more things from home to burn, like DVDs of *Dumbo* and books from the Babar series. Many husbands were gleefully disposing of their wives' collections of young adult vampire fiction. A group of women to Marvin's right stood with their arms around one another's shoulders, quietly sobbing.

And on top of the pile, positioned almost as though the rally's organizers knew where Marvin would be standing, was the latest issue of Fearless Phil. Marvin was all for public hysteria—when it kept the attention of his fellow students directed away from him—but he couldn't abide the destruction of perfectly good comic books.

"Looks like you'll have to wait a bit to talk to Constance," Marvin's dad said, pointing to the stage at the far end of the park. They could see Constance Upton mounting the stairs, along with the mayor and his advisors.

The crowd grew restless as the mayor approached the podium.

"What are we doing here?" someone shouted. "We're wasting our time!"

"Looks like the only thing you're good at is making speeches!" someone else yelled. "When are you going to catch this monster?"

"You still haven't fixed the potholes on my street, you bum!" A roar of assent went up from the crowd.

The mayor was sweating as he approached the microphone. "Citizens of Butcherville," he began, struggling to be heard over the crowd. "Noble and QUIET citizens of Butcherville, I come before you with good news."

"You're resigning?" someone shouted.

"I come before you to say that this terrible chapter in our town's history is finally coming to a close. I am proud to say that, due to the tenacity and bravery of our police force, in the past seventeen days there have been no more killings—THAT WE KNOW OF!" The crowd let forth a hopeful cheer at this. The mayor's face brightened, and he continued. "We come together tonight to let the Elephant Vampires of the world know that we stand united as a single mob!" The crowd cheered again. "And that this mob will *never* back down!" The cheering went on for a full minute before the mayor motioned Constance over to the podium.

He continued, "Tonight's celebration of unity and strength would not have been possible without the efforts of the Pork Loaf Ladies' Auxiliary, and especially the leadership of its beloved acting president, Mrs. Constance Upton!" Constance gave a gracious curtsy as the crowd cheered. Marvin's mom scowled a little and remained silent, cradling Baby Harry in her arms.

"Now," the mayor said, waving his hands for quiet, "I have listened long and hard to you, the citizens of Butcherville, during this time of trial. People tell me that big decisions are good. And for once, I wanted to make a big decision—all by myself. So, I called the governor of our great state, and demanded that he mobilize the National Guard to take action to protect our citizens. Using all of our resources, and yours, and making some educated guesses, we have tracked the Elephant Vampire to his lair. And now, everyone, please direct your attention toward the Butcherville Central Cemetery!" He pointed away to the north, and everyone's eyes followed. Over the loudspeakers came the sounds of classical music.

"Is that the *1812 Overture*?" Marvin's dad asked, cocking his head to listen. As the song reached its crescendo, a formation of fighter jets screamed overhead from the south. The mayor stood rigidly at attention, as much as his perpetually slumped shoulders would allow, and saluted the planes as they passed. A moment later, synchronized perfectly with the recorded music's cannon blasts, rockets streaked from the planes and a huge explosion lit the northern horizon. The jets peeled away from the billowing fireball that rose into the sky, and the crowd erupted into enthusiastic cheers as, in the distance, tombstones and bits of mausoleum rained down like confetti.

The mayor turned back to the microphone. "The Elephant Vampire is dead! Long live *us*!" The crowd cheered again, and Constance walked down to the

edge of the bonfire circle. A firefighter lit the sparkler in her hand, which she in turn gave to a small girl— the youngest member of the Little Ladies of Pork, the PLLA's junior group. She hoisted the smiling tot over the bonfire materials, and watched as the girl tossed the sparkler onto the gasoline-soaked books and wood. The flames spread quickly, and the crowd in the park applauded.

Marvin saw the fire reach the top of the pile and begin to consume his Fearless Phil comic. The edges of the cover curled and blackened, and Marvin saw Phil's smiling face vanish into a swirl of flame and ash. At least, he thought, Phil had been laughing in the face of fear, right to the end.

"One last thing," the mayor said, "before you get too caught up in hugging your loved ones and roasting some good old-fashioned Pork Loaf Franks." The crowd laughed. "I would like to announce, now that the crisis has passed, that the Harvest Festival, Parade, and Dance are all back on!"

The crowd shouted jubilantly. All except for Marvin. At the thought of the dance, he felt a sinking sensation in his stomach. And this time, no one—not the National Guard, not even Fearless Phil—could save him.

The mayor waved his arms dramatically, cueing someone behind him. Fireworks shot into the sky, and Marvin threw up in his mouth a little.

Interlude

High above the celebrating crowd, fireworks blossomed in blue and red and gold. Their light found its way far across town and through a cracked window, where the starbursts glinted in eight shiny eyes.

"Oh, oh hunger pangs," the spider groaned into the air of the darkened room where he lay hidden. "Oh wracking pain that makes me feel as though I have never tasted food! For nights uncounted have I stalked this town, only to find nothing. Nothing! No livestock, no wild beasts, no errant travelers. Only hunger. And SWAT teams." He had considered trying to feed on the helmeted, armored, and heavily armed police that had been scouring the town, but had rejected them on the basis that their shells would be too hard, and they too difficult to eat. "And me without a nutcracker!" he wailed.

His head drooped, and he continued, more quietly. "Nay, that is but vanity. Does fear unseat me? I,

Caliban, am powerful! For thus do I name myself, after the noble creature so many considered a monster. Yes, I am powerful, and yet—and yet—the specter of that elephant haunts me." He lifted the stump of his severed leg into the faint light shining through the window, and knew that it was fear, more than reinforced Kevlar body armor, that had kept him from taking on the SWAT teams. "Fie on thee, my tuskéd foe that hath maimed me thus, body and soul, and left me trapped here, famished, amid this waste and wreckage!" He swept a leg across a pile of debris, scattering objects across the wooden floor. "And curse the two-legged dullards that hunt me, denying me my nourishment. There is nothing to eat here. Nothing! A feast of dust and emptiness!" He picked up a tattered doll. "Oh, if only you were flesh and blood, my lovely. Alas, you appear to be filled with pine shavings." He threw the doll aside. Next he found a deflated football, and held it close to his face. "Oh, lowly pigskin! If only you held pig within!" He flung it away.

Overcome by despair and frustration, the spider collapsed to the floor and beat his legs. "Nothing! Nothing but scraps and tatters!" He picked a small

envelope off the floor in his fury, and raised it up, preparing to crumple it and cast it away, too. But just then, another explosion of fireworks outside the window lit up the room, and he noticed the writing on the envelope.

"Eh?" he said, bringing it close and opening it. "What's this?" He scanned the contents, then squealed with excitement. "Here! Here is the answer! What perfection! All those succulent little pigs, unguarded in their pen! A banquet, decked out in formal wear! And best of all—the poetry of it! The sheer poetry! Worthy of the Bard himself!"

The fireworks continued to burst outside, filling the sky with twinkling, multicolored stars. The spider turned his eyes toward the flashes in defiance. *"O malignant and ill-boding stars! Now thou art come unto a feast of death, a terrible and unavoided danger."*

He cackled. "Namely, me!"

14

The March toward Victory

Sunny skies and faintly crisp air greeted the people of Butcherville as they turned out along Hackett Boulevard for the triumphant Harvest Day Parade. The crowds stretched all the way down the parade route, from its starting point in the industrial district alongside the river on the west end; past the statue of Butcherville's founder, William Billy "Butch" Hackett, in the center of town; and finally to the fairgrounds out east, where cotton candy, midway games, and a Ferris wheel waited to receive them.

Families had staked their claims to sections of sidewalk and were already tailgating in adjacent parking lots, searing up a full array of Pork Loaf delicacies on portable gas and charcoal grills, when Marvin's family marched into Town Square. They were late: Baby Harry was spitting up again, so Marvin's mom had to change her blouse twice before they could leave the house. Now there were no open spots to be found, and the Watsons gazed dejectedly at the thick throngs of people.

Just when it looked as though they would be forced to head out to the edge of town in order to find an open spot, Fatima jumped up from near the review stand and waved at Marvin. Marvin, with the thought of the impending dance now weighing heavily upon his mind, sheepishly and determinedly looked the other way, ignoring her waves and cries. Mrs. Watson finally spotted her, and said, "Marvin, isn't that your little friend from the barbecue?"

"No," Marvin said. "I don't know—"

"Yes, yes it is!" Marvin's mom said. Marvin watched in horror as his mom waved back.

"It looks like they have some space," said Marvin's dad. "I bet we could set up right next to them. Come on!" He pushed through the crowd, Marvin reluctantly following.

"Thank goodness you're here," Fatima whispered to Marvin. "For the past half hour, I've had to listen to a recitation of the pros and cons of inflatable exercise balls for core-strength workouts. Ridiculous."

"Well, I certainly won't be talking about that," said Marvin.

"Foofie!" a slender blonde woman behind Fatima called. Fatima's face darkened at the sound of the nickname. The woman wore a stylish white fleece pullover and large designer sunglasses. "Introduce us to this handsome young man, Foofie."

"This is Marvin Watson," Fatima mumbled. "Marvin, this is my father and my stepmother."

"Oh my!" Mrs. Curie said, squealing with delight. "Not the same Marvin who's taking you to the dance, is it, Foofie?"

"Foofie?" Marvin asked. Fatima merely glared at him.

"Dance?" Mrs. Watson said. "I didn't know you were planning to go to the dance tonight, Marvin."

"Did I not mention that?" Marvin said. "I can't imagine why."

"Isn't it exciting?" Mrs. Curie said. "Their first real dance! I keep telling her that there's more to life than those little electronic doodads she's always playing with."

"Harry Watson," Marvin's dad said, extending his hand first to Mrs. Curie and then to her husband.

"I'm Saïd Curie, purveyor of fine promotional items," Fatima's dad replied. "What's your function in society, Harry?"

"Oh, I work in the lab at Pork Loaf," he answered.

"Fantastic!" Mr. Curie said.

"I'm Mary," Marvin's mom said, shifting Baby Harry so she could shake hands properly.

"Stacy Curie, purveyor of slimmer thighs and tighter abs," said Mrs. Curie, laughing.

"Come again?" said Marvin's mom.

"Pilates, dear," said Mrs. Curie. "I have a studio on the North Side. You should come by sometime for a free lesson. It'll help you lose that baby weight!"

"Thanks," Mrs. Watson said through clenched teeth.

"Come, sit!" said Mr. Curie. He unfolded several camp chairs that were imprinted with different corporate logos. "Try one of my fine promotional camp chairs." Marvin and his family sat down.

"You thirsty?" He pulled out an insulated travel mug and filled it from a large thermos of hot cocoa. He handed the mug to Marvin's mom.

"Oh, what's this?" Mrs. Watson said, looking at the corporate logo on the side. It read, "Roach Parade Scorched Earth Outdoor Bug Bomb." At the bottom of the mug was the warning "DO NOT USE INDOORS OR NEAR LIVING THINGS."

"They're one of my best customers," said Mr. Curie. "They let me keep the extras. I thought the 'Roach Parade' would be a festive accompaniment for today's Harvest Parade."

He reached into a large bag on the ground behind him. "Here! We have some special gifts for you. All of you."

Saïd plunked a large trucker hat on Marvin's dad's head. It read, "I'm Using *Un-Bald Me Now*—Grecian Hair Restoration Formula."

"Something more fashionably feminine for the lady!" Mr. Curie said, sliding a tennis visor emblazoned with the logo for Paul Bunion's Wart Remover onto Marvin's mom's head.

"And we wouldn't want those little toesies to get

cold now, would we?" Mr. Curie said, tickling Baby Harry's chin. He slid another pair of baby booties over Baby Harry's thick socks. The booties read, "Big Al's Crocodile Farm, Bayou View, LA."

"We couldn't possibly take all of this," Marvin's mom said.

"Nonsense!" Saïd replied. "I have plenty of extras. Besides, it's good for business to get my samples out there, so people can get a closer look at the fine, quality craftsmanship of my promotional items."

"But, how will we carry it all?" Marvin's mom said, desperately looking for a way out.

"Ah!" Mr. Curie said, reaching back into his stash. "The perfect tote bag." He handed Marvin's mom a cloth bag bearing a picture of the Pork Loaf Big 'Un and the text "Bag a Big 'Un!"

"Unfortunately, after the murder of our town's beloved elephant, the slogan seems a bit insensitive," Mr. Curie said sadly. Then, he brightened. "But now it's yours! Enjoy!"

In the distance, they could hear the sound of trumpets and drums as the parade approached. Marvin stood up out of his chair to get a better look. He tapped

Fatima on the shoulder. "Look! It's the high school marching band!"

She didn't even glance up. "I have a much better view than you," she said, pointing to the screen of her electronic tablet. "They're simulcasting from the Pork Loaf Blimp." Marvin glanced up to see the bright-pink corporate blimp in the sky. A frequent sight at football games, fund-raisers, and the past three presidential inaugurations, the airship was shaped like an enormous Pork Loaf Log Roll.

As the parade marched closer, Marvin saw that the grand marshal was none other than PLI's beloved corporate mascot, Mr. Piggly Winks. Every child in Butcherville knew the smiling face of Mr. Piggly Winks, a grinning, dapper cartoon pig whose image could be found on all of Pork Loaf's products—and the occasional tattooed bicep. He was normally depicted wearing a top hat and tails and carrying a gentleman's walking stick. Today, though, the costumed character of Mr. Piggly Winks strode ahead of the marching band decked out in a drum major's hat and uniform and twirling a glittering baton. As always, one eye was clenched shut in a perpetual wink. He and the band were followed by a series of floats. Marvin could overhear the play-by-play of TV news announcers from the live stream on Fatima's tablet.

". . . and as you know, Bob, everything on these floats must be made from Pork Loaf meat products."

"That's right, Kelly. More than twenty tons of Pork Loaf was used in the creation of these mobile works of art."

"And it won't go to waste! After the parade, all the floats are donated to charity," Kelly said.

"Boy, I'd love to be the lucky charity that gets that meat sculpture of Big 'Un! Hungry children could feast on that one for days!"

"The generosity of this town knows no bounds."

At last, Marvin saw the sculpture they were talking about. On the back of an approaching float, a man dressed like a lumberjack in plaid flannel was hacking apart a twelve-foot-high tower of meat with a chainsaw.

Marvin eyeballed the spectacle warily. "Is that really sanitary?" he said.

"Oh, get into the spirit," Saïd said. "Besides, a little unrefrigerated meat never hurt anyone."

"I'm pretty sure *that's* not true," Marvin said.

Fatima scowled. "Will you two be quiet? I'm trying to listen to this." She shook her head and turned back to the live stream.

"Bob, that man hard at work on this day of celebration is internationally renowned meat artist Byron Potluck."

"With a name like that, I bet he's a hit at church picnics! Ha, ha, ha!"

"I'm sure he is! And he's ready to hit the record books today, because his artistic medium is the single largest Pork Loaf Big 'Un ever produced. By the time the parade reaches the fairgrounds, he will have completed his life-size tribute to Butcherville's dearly departed elephant, Big 'Un."

"Just breathtaking, Kelly, truly. And look—riding on the float with him are none other than the Little Ladies of Pork."

As the float passed by, Marvin saw small girls perched on its edges, smiling and waving to the crowd.

They wore pink jumpers and hats, with merit-badge-covered sashes draped across their chests. The roar of the chainsaw temporarily drowned out the music of the marching bands, and Marvin stepped back to avoid a foot-wide slab of Pork Loaf that fell to the street as the sculptor worked. Hunks of meat littered the parade route behind the float, and juices sprayed out onto the crowd as the chainsaw shaped Big 'Un's legs and trunk.

"Here!" Mr. Curie said, pulling out more promotional items from his stock. "They said on the news this morning that the first three rows might get a bit wet!"

He tied hair salon smocks, printed with the words "To Hair Is Human, to Cut Divine," around Marvin's and Fatima's necks. As meat juices from the chainsaw sprayed across them, Saïd slapped shower caps on their heads.

"Dad!" Fatima said. "Quit helping!"

"Saïd," Mrs. Curie said. "Really, now. You're making her look like a sack of potatoes."

"Yes, but the cutest little sack of potatoes!" Mr. Curie said. "Isn't that right, my little potato?"

"I am NOT a potato," Fatima grumbled.

"Look!" Marvin's dad shouted, pointing. "The Eleven Benevolent Elephants!"

Down the street rolled an arrow formation of ten loudly roaring minimotorcycles, piloted by elderly men wearing dress suits and white ceramic elephant masks. They gunned their engines and popped wheelies in unison, to the delight of the crowd.

"Here come the members of the Eleven Benevolent Elephants Society, whose fund-raising efforts have benefited Butcherville's schools, hospitals, and veterans associations," said a TV announcer.

"That's right, Bob. The oldest philanthropic group in Butcherville, the Elephants were formed by returning World War II veterans from the 111th Airborne Division—the Fighting Elephants."

"I sure hope they can see through those eye holes!"

"Members of the society wear those elephant masks to keep their identities secret. They believe that charitable acts should be anonymous, and not undertaken for personal gain or glory."

The motorcycles broke formation and began weaving in and out among one another in complex patterns, sending the crowd into greater jubilation.

"Normally there would be eleven members of the group present, Bob, but as you can see, the last motorcycle has an empty sidecar, draped in black, in honor of our departed Big 'Un."

"That's right, Kelly. Even among the joyous festivities of the Harvest Day Parade, we must take time to remember the big heart of that giant pachyderm."

"Oh no," Fatima said, glancing back and forth between her screen and the real parade. Marvin craned his neck to see what she was looking at.

Following the Eleven Benevolent Elephants in the parade was a gleaming red convertible. Perched high on the backseat, waving to the crowd, sat Little Stevie Upton and Amber Bluestone. An enormous billboard truck following behind their car proclaimed, YOUR FUTURE HARVEST KING AND QUEEN.

"Why those presumptuous little—" Fatima said angrily.

Stevie spotted Marvin and Fatima in the crowd, and called out to his driver. "Slow down! I want to say hello to my friends."

The driver slammed on the brakes, causing an immediate pileup in the parade behind them. Marvin could hear the sounds of screeching tires and crunching wood as floats and cars stopped and careened into one another.

"Look, Amber," Stevie said, "it's Marvin and Fatima. You remember them, don't you?"

"Oh, I try to forget," Amber said. She and Stevie smiled as though they hadn't spent the last two and a half weeks in isolation because of their unbearable odor. Marvin sniffed the air, but all he caught emanating from Stevie's direction was the strong scent of cologne. It seemed he had been able to shed Lee's otherworldly stench at last.

"I see you two picked out matching trash bags for the dance," Amber said.

"It's a beauty parlor smock, if you must know," Fatima said.

"A beauty smock?" Amber said, still smiling her gleaming smile. "It doesn't seem to be working."

"Driver, any chance you could run these two down?" Stevie said, leaning forward.

"Yes, please do," Marvin muttered, thoroughly mortified.

"Sorry, sir," the driver replied.

Marvin's mom looked up from her conversation with Fatima's parents and spotted Stevie and Amber. "Oh, hello, Stevie!" she said. "Don't you two look nice."

"Hello, Aunt Mary," Stevie said with a smile. "Sharp visor! The color really complements your eyes."

"Why, thank you, Stevie!" Marvin's mom said.

"Well, we have to get going," Stevie said. He turned back and eyeballed Marvin, whose smock and shower cap were soaked in a meaty brine.

"Watson," Stevie said, shaking his head, "there's nothing I can do to you that you haven't already done to yourself." He leaned in close so only Marvin could hear. "But trust me, I will. And more." Stevie's perpetual smile went away as he continued, deadly serious. "I'm not stupid, Watson. I didn't win top honors at Swineheart Academy just because of my wealth and popularity. Although I am wealthy. And popular. You're messing with the total package here." He shoved a finger in Marvin's face. "I know that you and braceface here had something to do with what happened in science class, and I'm going to find out what and how. And when that happens, my weeks of stinky exile will look like a vacation compared to your fate."

Stevie settled back into the car and tapped the driver's shoulder, and the car sped off to catch up with the rest of the parade.

"What was that all about?" Mrs. Curie asked, puzzled.

"That," said Marvin, "was my life in a nutshell." He watched as the giant billboard truck rolled by, and when it passed, he was surprised to see, on the other side of the street, Lee Skluzacek staring back at him. Marvin gave a tentative wave, and for a moment, Lee looked as though he was going to wave back. But then his face darkened, and he grabbed his grandmother by the hand and walked off into the crowd.

Saïd Curie stared up at the blue sky and around at the joyful crowd and sighed in satisfaction. "What a beautiful day," he said. "I'm so glad that Elephant Vampire is finally gone. Bad for business."

"There's no proof that they actually got the Elephant Vampire, Dad," Fatima said. "All they did was bomb a cemetery. It's not like they found his body."

"Well, to be fair, they found lots of bodies," Mr. Curie replied.

"He could still be out there," Fatima said. She glanced sideways at Marvin. "Maybe living in someone's attic, for all we know. Waiting to kill them in their sleep."

"Maybe that wouldn't be so bad," Marvin said.

"Don't dwell on the negative, Foofie," Mrs. Curie said, putting her arm around Fatima's shoulders. "It'll give you wrinkles." She glanced at her slim designer watch. "We should get going. You kids need time to get ready. This is the biggest night of your young lives!"

Marvin and his family began to make their way out of the crowd. "I wish *I* had been in that cemetery last night," he said, glumly removing his shower cap and smock. As soon as Marvin had taken off the smock, Baby Harry turned his head and spit up on his big brother's shirt. In sympathy, no doubt.

15

The Wrinkle in the Plan

When they arrived home, Marvin's mom said to him, "Marvin, honey, you should have told me you were going to the dance. We could have gone shopping and picked you out a new suit."

Marvin was startled. "I have to wear a suit? This just keeps getting better."

"Wow, your first dance, huh?" Marvin's dad said. "Well, you kids have been pretty cooped up lately with all of this Elephant Vampire nonsense. I guess we can extend your curfew a bit to, oh, say, eleven o'clock?" He slapped Marvin on the back.

"Ten o'clock's fine, really," Marvin said, dreading the prospect of extending the uncomfortable evening by another hour. "Nine, even."

"Do you have flowers?" Marvin's mom asked.

"No?" Marvin said questioningly. "Do I need flowers?"

"You do if you want the girl to have a nice time."

"What if I don't care whether or not she has a good time?" Marvin asked.

"Oh, Marvin," his mom said, shaking her head and smiling. "You don't have to try to hide your first crush from your old mom. You two make such a cute little couple."

"What?" Marvin said. "We're not a couple. She's just my lab partner. This is all part of some experiment."

"Oh, I remember the first dance your father took me to," Marvin's mom said dreamily. "Wasn't that great, Harry?"

"Yes, great," Marvin's dad said absently. "Do you need money for tickets?"

"No, I got them already," Marvin said. "They're up in my dresser."

"Oh, look at the time!" Marvin's mom said. "Harry, he still needs flowers. Run to the store and get a bouquet; I'll use it to whip up a corsage." She turned to Marvin. "Go get your suit so we can steam out any wrinkles."

Marvin dutifully trudged up the stairs to the attic.

As he approached, he heard the distinct sounds of hammering and grunting.

"Hold still!" a voice shouted from beyond the door. Marvin entered to see Ahab holding a makeshift, half-assembled, three-tiered bunk bed straight above his head as Aristotle hammered together pieces of wood to brace it all. Abraham lounged on the top bunk, his feet dangling off the edge, while the other two struggled to build the bed beneath him.

"It's not level yet!" Abraham shouted. "This end has to go higher."

"You know, it would be easier if you weren't sitting on top of it!" Aristotle said.

"This is the best vantage point," Abraham replied. "Do I tell you how to do *your* job?"

"Yes!" Aristotle shouted back. "You just did!"

"What are you doing?" Marvin said.

"Haven't you ever seen construction before?" Abraham said.

"Yes, but why are you doing construction in my bedroom?" Marvin said. "In fact, why are you even still here? They bombed the cemetery last night. That should be the end of the Elephant Vampire, if there ever was such a thing."

"Maybe it is," Abraham said. "But I haven't seen his body yet. Until we do, we're staying put."

"How could there possibly be a body left after that explosion?" Marvin said. Then he shook his head. "Never mind. I don't have time for this right now. I just need to get my suit." He stepped gingerly over piles of lumber and rusty nails, and opened the wardrobe.

It was empty.

"Where is it?" he asked. "Where are all of my clothes?"

"Full of questions today, aren't you?" Abraham said.

Marvin glanced around the room and, to his horror, spotted one sleeve of his light-gray suit sticking out of the hole in the wall. The suit had been crammed into the hole, along with most of his other belongings, as part of the moths' barricade. He pulled it out, then numbly laid it flat on his desk, which was still covered with the moths' anti–Elephant Vampire battle plans. Saying nothing, he tried in vain to smooth the creases and crinkles with the palms of his hands.

Abraham scooted over to the other end of the bunk so he could see what Marvin was doing. "What are we looking at here?"

"This is my suit," Marvin said quietly.

"Boy, that's one wrinkled piece of junk," Abraham said. "You're not gonna wear that, are you?"

"I *was* going to wear it," Marvin said, slowly turning to face the moth. "I *have* to wear it. Tonight. But it's all wrinkled because you shoved it into a hole in the wall!"

"Hole, shmole," Abraham said, becoming indignant. He stood up on top of the bunk and pointed angrily at Marvin. "Don't bite off *my* head just because you can't take care of your things!"

Ahab grunted uncomfortably, flexing his four arms. "Stop . . . shifting . . . around up there," Ahab said. "I can . . . only hold this steady . . . if you don't move."

Aristotle said, "I think—" Then, when the bunk bed creaked ominously above him, he stopped midsentence and backed off to the far side of the room.

"I've had it with the three of you," Marvin said.

"You take my stuff, you break my stuff, and worst of all, you wrinkle my stuff!"

Abraham puffed himself up in anger. "It's all about you, isn't it, Pops?" he said, glaring down from the bed. "Well, I've had just about enough of your selfishness! It's time for some changes around here." He began stomping his foot in time with his words. "I'm—putting—my—foot—DOWN!"

The final stomp was too much. Ahab lost his grip, and the bunk beds crashed loudly to the floor in a twisted heap of lumber and insect appendages. As Ahab and Abraham groaned amid the wreckage, Marvin's mom called up the stairs. "What's going on up there?"

"Nothing," Marvin shouted back out of reflex. Barely able to contain his anger, Marvin clenched and unclenched his fists. "Maybe I should look into getting a bug zapper," he muttered to himself. He closed his eyes and took a deep breath.

"Listen," he said to the moths through gritted teeth. "All I need . . . are my tickets . . . for the dance. Then you three can go back to your faulty construction projects." He moved to get the tickets from his dresser, but stopped short. "Where are my tickets?" Marvin asked. "Where is my dresser?"

"I'm under it," Abraham grunted. Marvin now recognized his dresser drawer among the components of their makeshift bunk beds.

"You made my dresser into bunk beds," Marvin said flatly. "You are *stupid* moths."

"How dare you!" said Aristotle, coming out of the corner. "We are *superintelligent* moths."

"Oh yeah?" Marvin replied. He grabbed a flashlight from the moths' emergency kit on the floor and clicked it on.

"Ooh," the moths said in unison, following the light with their eyes as he waved it back and forth.

"Pretty light," the moths said.

Marvin turned the dancing beam on Aristotle. "Aristotle," he said slowly, in rhythm with the hypnotic swaying of the flashlight. "Where are my tickets?"

"I . . . do not . . . know," Aristotle answered, his head bobbing up and down and back and forth.

"Ahab," Marvin said, swinging the beam back to the largest of the moths, who had pulled himself free of the bunk beds' wreckage. "Where did you last see my tickets?"

"When . . . Abraham . . . was shoving them . . . through the barricade . . ." Ahab said.

"Hey!" Abraham said, protesting. "You can't do this! You can't interrogate us without a lawyer present. We've got—ooh . . . pretty light . . ." He trailed off as Marvin swung the beam at him.

Marvin clicked off the flashlight and slapped it down hard in anger on his open palm. "You invade my space. You dismantle my furniture. You eat my sweaters. You snore. You douse me in salad dressing. You act like paranoid babies with all of this Elephant Vampire insanity. And your arms are too short for your bodies."

"I do not snore!" Abraham said. "That's a bald-faced lie!"

"I've had it," Marvin said. "I'm done."

"Now, wait just a minute—" Abraham said.

"No!" Marvin interrupted, swinging the flashlight up and shining it into the moth's multifaceted eyes. "I don't want to hear it." He grabbed his rumpled suit, walked past the frozen moth, and then clicked the flashlight off again.

"You have your eviction notice," Marvin said, his back to the moths. "I want you out of here by the time I get home tonight."

"But you're our father," Abraham said. "That's abandonment!"

Marvin rolled his eyes. As he headed toward the door, he kicked Aristotle's homemade catapult. "Anti–Elephant Vampire catapults," he said with a huff. "Fatima was probably right—it's probably one of YOU THREE that's the Elephant Vampire. Everything bad started when you showed up."

He took another look at the ridiculous contraption, with its battered metal colander barely secured to the swing arm with some twisted wire. "On second thought, none of you could be the Elephant Vampire," Marvin said. "You're all too incompetent." He slammed the door behind him.

Marvin walked up to Fatima's house, flowers in hand, his suit thoroughly soaked from his mom's attempt to steam out the wrinkles. She had sprayed the problem areas with water, hoping it would help relax the fibers, but all it did was make the suit look blotchy. So she sprayed the entire suit down before she ironed it. And yet, somehow, the suit remained wrinkled. Now it was also warm and damp, and the wool exuded a faint smell of musty attic.

A heavy sensation of dread sat in Marvin's stomach like a Triple-Decker-Pork-Loaf-Patty-Melt from Sal's Diner over on Hackett Boulevard. He had tried everything he could think of to get out of this dance, but in the end, not even a citywide panic caused by a supernatural killer could stop it. He clomped up the two steps to Fatima's porch like a condemned man who had exhausted all his appeals. He heaved a great sigh, releasing the last of his hope with it, and rang the doorbell. Fatima's stepmother, Stacy Curie, opened the door, smiling as usual.

"Oh, hello, Marvin," she said. "Come in!" He thanked her and stepped into the house. "What a nice suit," she said. "Is the rumpled look back in?"

"At least for tonight," Marvin said.

"Foofie will be down in a minute," Mrs. Curie said. "She's been upstairs all afternoon making herself beautiful."

"I can imagine that would take some time," Marvin said.

"Have a seat in the living room," Mrs. Curie said. "I'll go get her."

Marvin sat down on the sofa, which was upholstered in an off-white fabric. He stared at the family photos above the mantelpiece while he waited. Most prominent were the photographs that showed Fatima from year to year as she was growing up, each with increasing layers of mechanical gear: a picture of her sitting on the floor one Christmas, thick glasses on her nose, a toy educational computer in her hands, and tiny gleaming braces on her teeth; one of her at her first dance recital, her brace-encumbered leg held proudly out from her side in a ballet pose; one of her performing at a piano concert, shortly after the time she must have received her first set of headgear; and a photo of her "roughing it" on a family camping trip, with fifteen different mobile phones, GPS trackers, and computer gadgets clipped on to her fishing vest.

"What do you think?" Fatima's voice called from behind him.

Marvin turned and stood up. "Oh," he said. "I

didn't hear you coming." Then he stopped, dumbfounded. The girl standing at the foot of the staircase resembled Fatima, but only in the most superficial way. Her dark eyes gleamed out from a clear face, unencumbered by glasses. Her hair was pulled up into an elegant twist on top of her head, free for once of the tangling constraints of her oversize headgear, which was nowhere to be found. Her wrist was decorated with only a slim gold ladies' watch; no calculator, no mobile phone, no music player. And he could see why he hadn't heard her coming: The silhouette of her pale-blue dress showed that she had taken off her noisy, clanking knee brace for the evening.

"Wow," Marvin said.

"Thanks," Fatima said, smiling shyly, her small braces sparkling.

"Where's your knee brace?" he asked.

"Oh, I can take it off for one night," she said, "just so long as we don't get too 'jiggy' with our dance moves." Then she squinted at him closely. "Why are you all wet? Did you sit on our couch like that?"

Marvin glanced at the damp outline of his body on the sofa's upholstery. "No?" he said lamely.

"Is it raining outside?" she asked.

"My mom had to steam the wrinkles out of my suit."

"Well, she missed the wrinkles!"

"It was more wrinkled before."

"How could it possibly be more wrinkled? You look like a shar-pei!"

Just then, Mrs. Curie came into the hallway with a camera. "Picture time!"

"Oh, good," Marvin muttered. "I was hoping to immortalize this moment."

Marvin gingerly pinned the corsage his mom had made to Fatima's dress, without incident. He heaved a sigh of relief—then yelped as Fatima plunged a hatpin into his chest.

"Watch it!" Marvin said.

"Sorry," Fatima said, holding his boutonniere and squinting. "I can't see very well right now."

"I thought you were wearing contacts!" Marvin said.

"I don't own contacts," Fatima said, blushing slightly. "My parents never thought I was old enough to have them." She approached him with the pin and boutonniere once again.

She got it on the fourth try.

Fatima's stepmother arranged the two of them for the photo, placing Marvin's soggy arm around Fatima's shoulders.

"That better not leave a mark on my dress," Fatima whispered to Marvin through smiling, clenched teeth as the camera flashed.

16

The Dance

For the students of Butcherville Middle School, there was never a night as marvelous and mystical as their first Harvest Dance. Marvin knew *he* would remember this night forever. It was the night he discovered how long it took pants to dry while wearing them. The answer: longer than you'd like. Marvin had been walking with his hands in his pockets all the way from Fatima's house, but had to take them out when he discovered they were getting wrinkly from the dampness. Though his socks and underwear had been dry when he put them on, they were now thoroughly soggy, too, from contact with the wet pants. Worst of all, the suit's wrinkles persisted. Marvin hoped that the darkness of the dance floor would hide the magnitude of his disarray.

As they walked up the driveway to school, Marvin and Fatima could feel the thumping of the bass and see flashing lights through the high windows of the cafetorium. Cars passed on their way to drop off kids at the school entrance. Marvin paid the other students little mind, focused as he was on his wet, chafing clothes. But just then, a horn honked behind them.

Marvin and Fatima turned to see the Uptons' large black car pulling up beside them. "Hey, hot stuff," Little Stevie said as he climbed out of the car. "What are you doing with my loser cousin? How much did he pay you to be his date? Oh wait, he can't pay you. He's poor."

"Not all of us have to buy our friends, Stevie," Fatima said.

A look of shock spread across Stevie's face as he recognized her, but it quickly turned to amusement. "Hey! It's nerd-bot! You look good without that lobster trap on your face." Fatima blushed.

Amber Bluestone followed Stevie out of the car. "Oh, Stevie," she said, "I'm sure that horrid girl doesn't want your pity. It's your cousin who deserves our pity. Can't you see he's distressed?" She looked at Marvin with false sympathy in her eyes. "Why the long face, sweetie? Is it your crappy suit?"

Marvin felt too defeated to come up with a smart response.

"Enough hobnobbing with the peasants," Stevie said, taking Amber by the arm. "Our coronation awaits."

Stevie and Amber cut past the line of students waiting to check in at the door, tossing a wink and a smile to the chaperones and entering immediately. After a few more minutes, Marvin and Fatima found themselves at the front of the line, where their librarian, Mrs. Goudy, was collecting tickets.

"Oh, hello, Marvin. Hello, Fatima," she said, smiling. She checked their names off a list in front of her. "Do you have your tickets?"

"Not exactly," Marvin said. "I sort of lost them."

"You what?" Fatima said, turning on Marvin. "After all my reminders? You *do* know we need tickets to get in, right?"

"I'm sure it won't be a problem," Marvin said. "Right, Mrs. Goudy?"

"Ohhhhh," Mrs. Goudy said, the smile leaving her face. "I'm sorry, Marvin. We can't let you in without a ticket."

"But I bought the tickets from *you*," Marvin said. "In person. And our names are on the list."

"Marvin, Marvin, Marvin," she said, shaking her head sadly. "I would love to let you in. But don't you know that the rule of law is the only thing that separates man from beast? That distinguishes us from the Elephant Vampires of the world? Unless you have two dollars per person, I can't let you through."

Marvin eyed the line that was piling up behind them. "All right, well, I *think* I have enough." He began to dig in his pants pockets, pulling out handfuls of mixed coins and dumping them out on the table.

"Oh, thank you, Marvin," Mrs. Goudy said. "We needed more change."

"I have a five right here—" Fatima tried to cut in.

"No, it's all right," Marvin said. "I've got it."

The line continued to grow behind them, as did the angry murmurs. Marvin fished the last stray pennies out of his pocket and plunked them on the tabletop. "There," he said. "Four dollars. You don't have to count it."

"Rule of law, Marvin, rule of law," Mrs. Goudy said as she stacked the coins in small piles. She tallied them all, then paused. "I'm sorry, Marvin. That's only three ninety-eight."

"That's disappointing," Marvin said. Fatima hid her face in her hand.

Marvin turned his pocket inside out and saw that there was a tiny hole in the bottom.

"Wait a minute," he said. "I think some of the coins may have fallen down into my shoe." He pulled off his right shoe and began to peel the wet sock off his foot.

Mrs. Goudy held up her hand. "Three ninety-eight will be fine," she said.

The mirrored disco ball splashed spinning droplets of light onto the dance floor, where a few brave souls were hopping in time to the music—a lively pop number. Others milled around and talked, while a number of shy students clustered in gender-segregated groups at either end of the cafetorium and eyed the opposite sex suspiciously. Chaperones—teachers and parents— mingled throughout the room, mostly ignoring the kids and chatting with one another. A long table covered with white linen and laded with hors d'oeuvres sat against the far wall; its centerpiece was a four-foot-tall sculpture of Mr. Piggly Winks, carved entirely out of Pork Loaf by Byron Potluck himself. Just overhead, pink and white streamers twisted lazily through the air, while far above, the ceiling's beams and rafters were lost in shadow.

"So what do you want to do?" Marvin asked.

"I'm glad you asked," Fatima said, pulling a folded-up piece of paper from her purse and handing it to Marvin. "Here's the itinerary."

Marvin unfolded the page and scanned it. It was a minute-by-minute schedule of the entire evening.

"Why don't you read that and tell me where we stand," she said. "I can't see anything without my glasses. You'll also, possibly, have to tell me where things are situated and who people are. But we can get to that later."

"According to this, we're already behind schedule," Marvin said. "We should be well into the early up-tempo dancing by now." He tucked the list into his pocket.

"Good," Fatima said. "Have you practiced your dance moves?"

"I thought I'd just squirm around a little. How does that sound to you?"

"Fine. Fine," she said, scanning the room with squinty eyes. "If I remember correctly, it goes up-tempo dancing, followed by exhilaration and slight breathlessness, then picture-taking, salty snacks, punch, schmoozing with likely voters, bathroom break, more up-tempo dancing, more exhilaration, slight sweating, I trip on the hem of my dress, you catch me gallantly, our eyes meet, we glimpse a possible future together, you moisten your lips, I smile slightly, the music slows, hearts flutter—"

"This is a gruesome blow-by-blow," Marvin interrupted. "Where are you going with this?"

"Well, what's on the list after 'hearts flutter'?" Fatima asked.

"Um—" Marvin said, pulling out the list and looking closely at it again. "My damp suit sort of smeared the ink," he said. "I guess we'll have to improvise."

Fatima sighed. "If you continue to behave like this, we don't have a chance of being voted king and queen and beating your smug little cousin."

"Behaving how?" he said. "Behaving wetly?"

"Let's just dance," she said.

They went out on the floor, dancing and squirming to a number of songs, before stopping to have their picture taken by the professional photographer. They sampled the various hors d'oeuvres, all of which were made with Pork Loaf, including pigs in blankets, Pork Loaf pâté on crackers, Pork Loaf fondue, and even edible flowers made from sculpted Pork Loaf fondant. Since they were still running behind schedule, Fatima decided they should combine agenda items, so she and Marvin sipped on their grape Pork Punch while they were schmoozing with their fellow voters.

"Who's that?" Fatima whispered to Marvin.

"That's Eugene Peters," Marvin said.

"You mean Pee-Pee Peters?" Fatima said, wrinkling her nose. "Back in third grade, he was wetter than you are now."

"I didn't need to know that," Marvin said.

"I just mean we have to concentrate our lobbying efforts on the power players and social connectors," Fatima explained. "Who's that?"

"That's a folding chair," Marvin said. "I think we can skip that one."

"How about him?" Fatima asked, squinting.

"That's Brett Rollingsford," Marvin said.

"Perfect!" she said. "Take me over there."

Marvin grabbed her elbow and steered her around people and furniture until they reached Brett, a tall, blond-haired soccer player who was chatting with several good-looking girls. He glanced up in some surprise at Marvin and Fatima.

"Hi, Brett!" Fatima said, smiling cheerfully.

"Uh, hi—" Brett said, clearly not recognizing her.

"It's me, Fatima! Fatima Curie."

"Um—"

"I'm the one who complains all the time in social studies class!"

"Oh!" he said. "Right. Hi."

"As you know, I've been nominated for Harvest Queen this year."

"Really?" Brett said. "Who nominated you?"

"Oh—admirers," she said. "Anyway, I sure hope I can count on your vote tonight."

"Why should I vote for you?" Brett asked.

"I think we can all agree that a Harvest Queen should have both beauty *and* brains," Fatima said.

"Hunh," Brett said noncommittally. "Never thought of that."

"Well, you're thinking *now*, Brett," she said, "and that's what counts."

He glanced over at Marvin. "And who's the wet mop?"

Marvin shifted uncomfortably. "I'm Marvin Watson. I'm her date, I guess."

Brett eyed Marvin's wrinkled suit for a long moment before turning to leave. "Hate to tell you this, sweetie, but that limp rag on your arm is holding you back." He walked off with the other girls, who giggled and whispered as they went.

Fatima watched them, openmouthed, as they walked away.

"That's enough of the campaign trail for me," Marvin said. "I think I could use some more punch."

"What? You can't leave," Fatima said, turning to face him. "You're part of this ticket!"

"I don't know how much more abuse I can take in a single night," Marvin said. "And you don't need me. You heard what he said—I'm just dragging you down." He stared at his wrinkly sleeves and sighed. "I wouldn't have even come in the first place—heaven knows I did everything I could to get out of it—but I knew this meant a lot to you. I didn't want to disappoint you."

"Well, you're doing a really lousy job of it!" she said.

"Look, this isn't my world," Marvin said. "And it's not yours, either. You may be able to take off the glasses and headgear, but underneath, you're still you—and they know it."

"Oh yeah?" Fatima shouted angrily. "Well, tonight I'm not me! I'm *better* than me! And I'm going to *win* that crown, with or without your help!" She turned and stormed off. Marvin watched as she started to introduce herself to another potential voter.

"You're talking to a potted plant!" Marvin called to her.

"I knew that!" she said, flushing, and walked across the room, out of his sight.

Marvin, not sure where to turn, decided to visit the bathroom to gather his wits. After he had finished and washed up, he ran his hands underneath the hot-air dryer. It then occurred to him that hot air could dry more than just hands, and he began drying his suit.

First one sleeve, then the other. Next the left pant leg, then the right. Eventually, he was shaking and wiggling his entire body beneath the warm jet of air like some wrinkly limbo dancer. He finally turned around completely to dry the seat of his pants, and discovered that someone had been waiting to use the dryer.

It was Lee. He stared stonily at Marvin, who was shaking his butt underneath the hot air.

"What happened?" Lee asked. "Did you fall in?"

"I—my suit—there were these—" Marvin stammered. "It's a long story."

Lee walked up and wiped his hands dry on Marvin's lapel. "You might need another minute under there now," Lee said, then walked out the door.

"Lee, wait!" Marvin yelled, running after him.

He caught up to Lee in the hallway and ran in front of him to stop him from walking away. "Lee, I'm sorry," Marvin said.

"Do you even know what you're apologizing for, Marvin?" Lee asked.

"I'm sorry . . . that you're mad at me?" Marvin responded lamely. Lee just rolled his eyes. "Well, what's it going to take?" Marvin asked. "How long is this going to go on? Do you think you'll get over it tonight? I don't have anyone to hang out with here."

"Sorry I'm ruining your plans," Lee said. "What happened to your *date*?"

"Fatima?" Marvin said. "She's too busy climbing the social ladder to hang out with the likes of us."

"What *us*?" Lee said. "I only see *me* and *you* here. You proved that when you were willing to blow me up to get back at your cousin." Lee stepped around Marvin and walked back toward the cafetorium.

Marvin watched him go. "You smell better!" he shouted.

Marvin stood alone in the hallway, recounting the evening's misfortunes. Fatima had abandoned him in pursuit of fame. Lee wanted nothing to do with him. And most of the school thought of him as a laughing-stock. Even the moths would no longer be on speaking terms with him when he returned home. Here he was, only weeks into the school year, left friendless and alone.

Marvin felt a chill go through his bones.

It was then that he realized his underwear was still slightly damp.

As he went back to dry his underwear, Marvin muttered to himself, "This night could not possibly get any lousier." He brushed aside a large, hanging cobweb on his way into the bathroom.

Interlude

"That kid is mentally unstable," Abraham said as he hauled boxes out of Marvin's room and into the moths' old attic space. "Like all children." He hadn't stopped ranting since Marvin had stormed out. "The very idea that one of us is the Elephant Vampire. Preposterous! Sickening! Bigoted!"

"Bigoted?" Ahab asked.

"Anti-insectian!" Abraham said.

"I don't think that's a word," Ahab said.

Abraham continued, unfazed. "I mean, Ahab, you're clearly big enough to wrestle an elephant into submission, but why would you? Unless it was simply to quench your bottomless hunger for blood and destruction!"

"I don't follow," Ahab said, and scratched his head.

"Or you, Aristotle," Abraham said, whirling to face the tall, skinny moth. "You are certainly smart enough to rig up a contraption that could suck the fluids from the body of some poor victim, but to what end? Sure, your twisted sense of scientific curiosity knows no bounds or reason, but look at your spindly limbs—you're far too feeble to subdue a wild beast. Why, you'd need an assistant to hold down your victims. An assistant powerful of body but possessing meager intelligence—" He gasped. "It's the two of you together, isn't it! A vampiric duo—and me, the patsy!"

"Patsy? Well, I won't argue with that last bit, you dolt," Aristotle said.

"What's he talking about, Aristotle?" Ahab asked.

"It seems our comrade believes that you and I are actually the Elephant Vampire," Aristotle said. "That *we* are responsible for the terrifying rash of killings around Butcherville."

"That doesn't sound like something I'd do," Ahab said, puzzled.

"No, my dear Ahab, you are far too gentle of heart to fit the profile," Aristotle said. "The deeds of the Elephant Vampire could only have been carried out by a maleficent individual, steeped in hate and foul of breath. Driven to homicidal madness by a Napoleon complex caused by his own rage and self-loathing over his short stature."

"Hey, wait a second," Abraham said, waggling a claw at the much taller moth. "I see where you're going with this."

"Astonishing," Aristotle said calmly. "I didn't think you had the wit."

"Hey, relax, guys," Ahab said, stepping between the two. "None of us is the Elephant Vampire."

"How can you be so sure?" Abraham said.

"Because we're all friends!" Ahab exclaimed cheerfully.

"That makes no sense!" Abraham said, but his protests were soon squeezed out of him as Ahab embraced his fellow moths in a crushing group hug.

"Good times," Ahab said as he—eventually—released them. "I kind of miss Marvin, though. It's sad we won't see him anymore."

"If anyone's a vampire, it's that kid," Abraham grumbled. "I mean, look how pasty he is. And that hair—you can tell he's never looked in a mirror."

The moths continued moving boxes and furniture back through the hole in the wall from Marvin's room to their own attic. Abraham carried a box full of Marvin's wool sweaters into the room—"the spoils of war!" he had declared—and began sorting them by flavor and country of origin.

Ahab came in carrying four overloaded boxes in his various arms. "Where should I put these?" he asked.

"Just stick 'em anywhere," Abraham said, not looking up from his unpacking.

Ahab walked toward the dark corner farthest from Marvin's room. "Should I put them here by the wall, or over here next to this great big pile of bones and skin?"

"By the wall," Abraham said. "Wait a minute. Bones and skin? What did you move those in here for?"

"Let me see," Aristotle said, putting down the TV he had been carrying with a loud thump. He walked over and peered at the pile of grisly remains. "Hmm. Murine. Feline. Vulpine. Canine. Porcine. Bovine. All desiccated."

"What, is the kid taking up taxidermy in his spare time?" Abraham asked.

"I don't think so, Abraham," Ahab said, shaking his head slowly. "These carcasses were already here when we came back through the barricade."

"Well, who else but a taxidermist is going to suck all the blood out of someone and leave behind a dried-up corpse?" Abraham said.

"Is it not obvious?" Aristotle said. "We are standing in the lair of the Elephant Vampire. He has been living under this very roof all along."

Ahab shrieked and fainted, cracking several low rafters and tearing a large hole through the roof as he fell backward.

Aristotle sighed. The tall, thin moth then stooped over and examined what were apparently the Elephant Vampire's personal effects. He picked up a large, cloth-bound volume from the floor.

"Aha," he said. "*The Collected Works of Shakespeare.* We are dealing with a sophisticated foe. I fear this will not be easy."

"Easy?" Abraham said. "What are you talking about? Running away and hiding is real easy!"

Aristotle ignored him and continued his examination. Tucked into the pages of the book were two slips of paper. "The banquet scene from *Macbeth*," Aristotle said, noting their location. "And look!" He held the makeshift bookmarks up to the light. They were

Marvin's missing tickets to the Harvest Dance. Words had been scrawled boldly across the face of one:

The feast begins at eight o'clock!

"So?" Abraham asked.

"So, it is clear that the Elephant Vampire is headed for the school right now, and he intends to devour all the children—including our friend Marvin!"

"You mean *former* friend," Abraham said, folding both sets of arms. "Better him than me."

"Now that's just mean," said the giant Ahab, who was staggering to his feet. "He let us move into his room when we were all worried about the Elephant Vampire, and he's been good about bringing us sweaters to eat, even if they are a little stale. I'm going to help him."

Ahab riffled through one of the boxes and pulled out his "Kiss the Cook—OF DEATH!" apron. He tied it around his enormous abdomen and began stuffing the pockets with weaponry: spatulas, whisks, a rotary egg beater, a can of nonstick Pork Spray, and some sharpened chopsticks.

"Up, up, and away!" he shouted, running full tilt toward the new hole in the roof and leaping into the air.

His flight ended with a loud crunch, as his body became lodged halfway through the too-small opening.

"Well, that was anticlimactic," Abraham said.

"A little help down there?" Ahab said, his voice muffled. "I think I need a boost!"

Aristotle sighed and shook his head. He wandered over to a corner and picked up a plunger. "This is good for getting clogs unstuck." He placed the red rubber of the plunger against Ahab's butt and began shoving vigorously until Ahab finally popped out the other side in a shower of splinters and roofing shingles. Aristotle and Abraham heard him clatter down the roof with a grunt and a cry of alarm before he got his wings going. Then they watched as the gargantuan moth buzzed unsteadily off into the moonlight.

"Hmm," Aristotle said, examining the newly enlarged hole in the roof. "An interesting turn of events. Yes, it should be big enough now." He dragged his spaghetti-strainer catapult across the floor and shoved it through the hole, climbing out after it.

"What the heck are you doing?" Abraham asked. "We don't need to store that thing outside. There's plenty of room in here."

Aristotle looked back at him. "You may not under-stand this, being the intellectually bereft tyrant that you are, but as a creature of science, I need to know that my invention works. And this battle is the perfect test case. At last, I shall face a foe worthy of my genius. Plus, I am worried about Ahab. And Marvin." He raised his wings into position. "I bid you a less-than-fond farewell." He flew off into the night, though perhaps less gracefully than he would have liked, weighed down as he was by his siege engine.

"Thanks for leaving me in the Elephant Vampire lair alone! Maybe to die! Alone!" Abraham stuck his head through the hole in the roof. "Did you hear me? Hello? I'm berating you!" He grabbed an old wooden baseball bat and then jumped out and took wing after them. "You won't get rid of me that easy! I'm not through with you yet!"

17

The Return of the King

As Marvin, dry for the first time in hours, walked back into the cafetorium, he saw that Mrs. Goudy was standing on the dais, talking to the DJ. The DJ nodded and picked up his microphone as the song ended.

"Okay, little party people!" he said, getting the room's attention. "This is it! The moment you've all been waiting for! It's time to rock and roll your body and soul, to gather round and get down—there's gonna be uproarium in the cafetorium when we crown the Harvest King and Queen!"

The kids drew in around the dais, murmuring in excitement. Marvin stopped off at the back table for another glass of punch and then stood at the outer edge of the crowd.

"Now, listen up, you groovy cats and catstresses! Er, kittens. Whatever! Let me turn the mic over to your mistress of ceremonies!" the DJ continued.

"That's right! It's gonna get rowdy, 'cause here's Chrysanthemum Goudy!"

"You don't need to do that," Mrs. Goudy said as she took the microphone. "I really don't care for nonsensical chatter. Words should mean something. Just do your job."

"Yes, ma'am!" the DJ said with the same smile and enthusiasm.

"While, intellectually, I am opposed to this entire evening," Mrs. Goudy announced to the crowd, "I will complete my duties as your head chaperone to demonstrate how responsible adults should behave."

She looked over a list in her hand. "Let's have all the nominees come up. First, we have Amber Bluestone, accompanied by Stephen Upton Jr."

There was applause and wild hooting and hollering from Stevie and Amber's friends. Marvin watched the crowd part as the couple made their way up to the stage, waving and smiling as if they had already won. Then he felt someone seize his arm in a painful, vise-like grip. It was Roland Offenbach, Stevie's enforcer. "Cheer for Stevie, or you'll be wearing that punch," he said.

"Normally, I might refuse, but I just spent two hours drying my suit," Marvin said. He cradled his glass of punch in the crook of his arm and clapped politely, glancing nervously over at Roland.

Mrs. Goudy went on. "Next, we have Tilly Hoefecker, accompanied by Cary Papadopolis." More cheers came from the crowd.

Roland looked over at Marvin. "You can stop cheering now," he said.

"You know, I'm not some cheer machine you can just turn on and off at will," Marvin said.

"What's that supposed to mean?" Roland asked, frowning.

"Exactly," Marvin said.

"Just watch yourself, Watson," Roland said. He put two fingers to his own glaring eyes and then pointed them at Marvin, before turning and walking up closer to the stage.

"That's you watching me," Marvin said, "not me watching my—oh, forget it."

Onstage, Mrs. Goudy continued to read the names of the court. "Felicity Rushmore, accompanied by Paul Thackerman," she said. When the clapping died down, she added, "And, lastly, Fatima Curie, accompanied by . . ." Mrs. Goudy paused as Fatima ran up to the stage, hurriedly whispering something to her. The librarian nodded, then said, "Fatima Curie." Fatima strode confidently around the front of the dais to the steps, waving to the people and smiling.

Marvin began to feel a bit sheepish at leaving Fatima to face this alone. He looked around at the crowd. Few were cheering. Most chuckled and giggled. Marvin clapped loudly and cheered, "Woo-hoo!" But up on stage, Fatima didn't quite know how to take his enthusiasm; mostly, it seemed to remind her that he had abandoned her, and her beauty-queen smile became strained.

"Let's hear a round of applause for your Harvest Dance Court," Mrs. Goudy said. "And although only one couple will be crowned king and queen of this Paleolithic popularity contest, I want to say that you are all kings and queens in my book."

"Books are for losers!" Roland shouted. "Get to the point!"

"Yeah, if we could speed things along, that would be great," Stevie said. "I've got a victory party to get to after this and a ribbon-cutting with the mayor tomorrow!"

Mrs. Goudy narrowed her eyes at him but continued in her duties. "Very well," she said as she opened an envelope containing the winners' names. "The king and queen of this year's Harvest Dance are—"

The room fell silent. Amber reached her hands out expectantly to receive her award.

"—Stephen Upton Jr. and Amber Bluestone!" Mrs. Goudy finished. "Well that's a surprise," she muttered.

Mrs. Goudy placed the tiara in Amber's hair, and the crown atop Stevie's head. Amber hugged each of the other nominees, and Marvin saw that Fatima's smile looked even more strained.

"Now," Mrs. Goudy said, "the king, queen, and their Harvest Court will dance to a soulful rendition of our school fight song—successfully lobbied against and changed by yours truly into a safety message, and sponsored, despite my protests, by Pork Loaf International . . ." She paused to take a breath. "A song led by three-time regional runner-up for that inane television reality show where they all sing—our own Christina Carlucci!" She handed the microphone over to a wholesome-looking girl with long, curly hair, and the DJ cued up the backing track, which was the melody to "America (My Country, 'Tis of Thee)":

Butcherville Middle School,
Obey the cardinal rule:
Keep hands inside!
When you are on the bus
Don't get your hands cut off;
You'll cause an awful fuss.
Please buy Pork Loaf!

The students stood at attention, their hands over their hearts, surrounding the dance floor where Stevie, Amber, and the other couples stepped and swayed to the music, which was totally unsuited to dancing. Fatima stood by herself, twirling idly in circles, as she had no dance partner. Her forced smile gradually gave way to a look of utter dejection.

As the song ended, Mrs. Goudy once again took up the microphone. "And now, I'd like to introduce a woman who stands in opposition to everything I believe," she said. "To present our winners with a special prize, here is the reigning Miss Pork Loaf USA, Crystal Sherwood."

"Thank you for that warm introduction," Crystal said breathlessly, leaning into the microphone. "It is my honor to present our king and queen with this Porkucopia, filled with enriched meat products, each of which I fully endorse. May your reign be marked by peace and justice, and the American way." The students cheered as the blonde pageant winner handed Stevie and Amber the three-foot-long horn of plenty, which was overflowing with cans of various Pork Loaf products. "And now," Crystal continued, "my trusty assistant will hand out summer sausages to the runners-up." The beauty queen turned to Mrs. Goudy.

"I'd really rather not," the librarian said, eyeing the second-place prizes. "I'm a vegetarian. I'm doing all I can not to gag here." But Miss Pork Loaf USA raised a perfectly groomed eyebrow at her, and Mrs. Goudy sighed and did her duty. She passed a plastic-wrapped, foot-long sausage to each of the remaining candidates. She came to Fatima last. "Since you don't have an escort, you can have two, dear," she said.

"I don't even want *one*," Fatima said as she accepted the two hunks of cured, shelf-stable meat and walked off in a daze. She pushed through the crowd and headed across the room, then sat in a folding chair far away from the action, where she could be alone. She took little notice of Lee, who was glumly eyeing the hors d'oeuvre table—everything was made of Pork Loaf, so there was nothing for him to eat—or of Marvin, who watched the two of them from the edge of the crowd, unsure of what he should do to make things right.

Back on the stage, Stevie took the microphone to give his acceptance speech. "My fellow middle school-erians," he began. "Our town has been through a tough time lately. I, myself, was forced to take a difficult journey. To walk through the valley of the smell of death. But I have come through to the other side"—some heads in the crowd began to nod—"stronger than before!" Stevie said, louder.

It was true, Marvin had to admit to himself: Stevie had come out of it all smelling like a rose. How could it be that two people, both from the same family, could have lives that followed such different trajectories? While Marvin's own fortunes were at their lowest point, he stood and watched his cousin glory in his seemingly inevitable triumph.

"And you, too, have walked a difficult road these many weeks!" Stevie continued. "Difficult not only for the absence of our guidance, but because you were forced to live under the cruel reign of the Elephant Vampire. You faced a threat, not only to your lives, but to your deepest principles. In that dark hour, you looked to the skies for deliverance, and you saw *us*! In this, our coronation, you have found your new hope!"

He paused to bask in the cheers and adulation of his subjects. "As your new king, I promise you not just better days for *all*, but better days for *some*!" Stevie waited for the applause to die down, and continued more quietly, as if confiding in the crowd. "You see, somewhere along the line, we lost our way. That is why we must return to the values of our forefathers, who didn't judge a man's worth by his accomplishments, or by how much he knew, but by how popular he was!"

The crowd cheered again. "The way will not be easy. It will require much sacrifice—mostly by you! Separately, our selfish endeavors mean nothing, but together, our selfish endeavors mean everything! I leave you with this thought: Benevolence is overrated, but a lifetime is forever! Thank you."

"'A lifetime is forever,'" Marvin muttered. "Yeah, especially when it's filled with shame and ridicule. And wrinkly clothes."

In the back of the room, Lee sneered at Little Stevie's speech. "'The absence of your guidance'?" he said, to no one in particular. "It was only last week you were looking to *me* for guidance."

Just then, Olivia Muntz—one of his former Odiferous Needs classmates—walked up to the hors d'oeuvre table to get some punch.

"Hey, Olivia," Lee said. "Some speech, huh?" Olivia barely glanced at him as he spoke. The music kicked up again, and the rest of the kids started to dance.

Lee bobbed his head to the beat. "Great song, isn't it?" he said to her. "So, you want to maybe dance a little bit?"

Olivia paused and looked Lee right in the eye. "You're still in that place, Lee," she said. "I get it. But I have to go back to living."

Lee looked at the ground and nodded his head.

"But I won't forget you," she said. She raised her hand as if to touch him on the shoulder, then dropped it and walked away.

He watched her walk back into the jubilant crowd. "Great song, isn't it?" she shouted to her friends as she rejoined them.

Lee scowled. "I don't know why I even bothered to come tonight," he said to himself, shuffling his feet in annoyance. "The music is terrible, and nobody here even cares whether I live or die." He glared at the table full of Pork Loaf products, which seemed to taunt him. "And right now, I would *kill* for something to eat."

A large shape rustled in the shadows just overhead. "So would I," a menacing voice replied, followed by horrifying laughter.

18

The Doom of Us All

As anyone who has read a book knows, unless there is some violence at the end, you'll never remember the lesson. Unfortunately for Lee, the lesson in this case was that menacing inhuman horrors that lurk in the darkness are not to be trifled with.

The spider swooped down on his silken cord and smashed Lee across the temple with one of his forelegs, knocking him half-unconscious. The half of Lee that was still conscious yelled, "Help!" Amid the cheers of adulation for the new king and queen, Marvin and Fatima were the only ones close enough to hear him.

Marvin and Fatima had been told about monsters before, of course. All children had. But the monsters in stories go away when you close the book, and the monsters under your bed vanish when you turn the lights on. This monster was not going away. This one, blown up to enormous size as if by some accursed microscope, was visible in all his gory details, from his furry legs to his enormous fangs to his cold, unblinking eyes, which, at that moment, stared straight through Marvin.

"Oh—" Marvin said, dropping his punch and turning pale. "What—what is that?"

Fatima staggered up out of her folding chair and gasped as she squinted at the blurry shape. "Is that— it's a giant *Hogna helluo*!" she said. "A wolf spider!"

"What?" Marvin said. "But it's the size of a cow!"

"Or an elephant!" Fatima said, realization dawning at last. "That thing is the Elephant Vampire! It's still on the loose!"

Marvin couldn't believe what he was seeing. Moreover, he couldn't believe that the Elephant Vampire was real. And then the inevitable thought occurred to him, and as he turned to look at Fatima, he saw that she had come to the same conclusion.

"You," she said. "This is *your* fault, isn't it?"

"Did I not mention that there were *four* test tubes of Pork Punch?" Marvin said.

"You sure about that?" Fatima said. "Not five? Or six? Should I be waiting for a vicious inchworm to eat us? Perhaps a malevolent cricket with a short fuse?"

"Get in your I-told-you-so's now," Marvin said. "I hear in the next life, we have to be nice to each other."

"I told you so," Fatima enunciated, slowly and deliberately.

"Really?" Marvin said, shaking his head and turning back to face the spider.

People don't know what they are capable of until thrust into a life-and-death situation. Does a person panic, or does he or she face the danger head-on? For Marvin and Fatima, it was a little of each. Fatima, having the most sense, stood rooted to the floor, staring at the spider in openmouthed horror as the seven-foot-tall killer looked her up and down hungrily with his many shiny eyes. Marvin, being somewhat stupider and more impulsive, charged the hors d'oeuvre table where the spider was gathering the limp body of Lee into his clutches.

"Lee!" he shouted, and jumped onto the table, grabbing a plastic spork on the way. In one fluid motion, he completed his charge and plunged the flatware deep into one of the spider's eyes. The glassy orb popped like a water balloon, but one that was filled with rot and venom, and the stench of the hundred victims the spider had consumed. Disgusting goo shot all over Marvin's wrinkled suit.

The spider shrieked and recoiled in pain, the spork still protruding from his eye. "You infantile ape!" the monster howled. "You ruined my perfect vision! I'll have your innards for soup!"

As Fatima realized she was about to witness the death of not one, but two of her friends (however unfriendly they'd been recently), every single emergency health and safety procedure that she had ever heard flashed through her brain: performing CPR. Splinting a broken arm. Recognizing the signs of heatstroke. Waiting an hour after lunch before swimming. Sitting at least six feet from the television. Chewing each mouthful of food thirty-two times. Keeping hands inside the bus. And calling 911.

"I've got to call 911!" she said, then remembered that she had left all her electronic communication devices at home. She patted herself from head to toe, but found only her corsage. She turned her tiny purse upside down, dropping a tube of lip gloss and a few dollars to the ground. "Stupid thing!" she said. "How do women fit cell phones in these?"

Fatima turned and ran toward the cheering crowd of students, all of whom had their eyes on Stevie and Amber and were utterly oblivious to the deadly struggle taking place on the opposite end of the cafetorium. She grabbed a girl on the dance floor by her bare shoulders and spun her around. "CALL 911!" Fatima shouted, receiving only a blank stare in return. Finally, she huffed in exasperation and turned to the girl's date. "Call the police!" The boy raised his eyebrows at Fatima and took a step back. Fatima glanced behind her and saw the spider recovering its balance. It wouldn't be long now. She turned back to the crowd and snatched the purse from a girl's hands.

"Hey!" the girl said. It was her fellow Harvest Court competitor Tilly Hoefecker, whose reddish-brown hair hung in frizzy curls around her shoulders. "What do you think you're doing, Fatima?"

"I need your cell phone," Fatima said, riffling through Tilly's purse. "It's an emergency!"

"Give it back, you freak!" Tilly said. She grabbed her purse and shoved Fatima to the floor. "You lost! Get over it! It's not an emergency. It's not even a surprise!"

Back at the table, Marvin cast about for another weapon. He pulled the metal ladle from the punch bowl and raised it up into a defensive position just as the spider started to advance again. He made a few halfhearted swings toward the spider's face, but the monster just stopped and laughed. "Oh, valiant indeed, my dear Knight of the Ill-Fitting Suit," the spider said. "I'll joust with you soon enough." The spider grasped tightly on to both Lee and the silken line. "But first, I'm going to savor this dainty appetizer!" He raced back up his webbing, Lee in tow, and vanished into the shadows overhead.

Marvin stared into the depths of blackness above, trying to make out any sign of movement, half-afraid that Lee was already being sucked dry like a freeze-pop. There was no way Marvin could get up there to help him.

No way, except the climbing rope from gym class, which was tethered to the cafetorium wall just above the far end of the table. Without stopping to think, he took a running leap and reached for the rope. His hands seized it, checking his forward momentum, and he swung around, straight into the wall. Marvin let out a grunt as he smacked into the painted cinder block, but kept his grip. He started climbing even before he had regained his balance.

As he passed the halfway mark, Marvin reflected on his earlier failure to climb the rope in gym class. This time, however, would be different. Lee's life was on the line, and Marvin had a chance to redeem himself—in front of the entire school, no less. That thought sent a warm feeling through his body. That feeling masked, for a few moments, the fact that his hands no longer seemed to be working properly. Then it was his forearms that began to quiver, and then his biceps. The warm feeling turned into a cold, sinking sensation in his stomach, as he realized that he lacked the strength to climb any higher. He was at a critical moment: Marvin knew that he could simply slide down to the floor and walk away from this with no more than the discomfort and indignity of rope burns on his thighs. But he would also be walking away from Lee. So he scrunched up his legs and gave one last upward push with all his might.

This proved to be a costly error.

Across the room, Fatima had regained her footing. She had also regained her inner fury. Like a
prophet of old, Fatima raised her hands above her head
and addressed the sea of students in a commanding
voice.

"Everyone!" she cried, and the nearer members of
the crowd turned their heads. "Heed my words! I call
upon you to witness this dread moment in history—to
witness our doom!"

"Grow up!" someone shouted back. "You lost the
contest!"

"Not my doom, you idiot," Fatima said, lifting her
index finger. "The doom of us all! Look where my finger points, because it points to your doom!"

All eyes in the crowd followed her finger, but they
alighted not upon the giant spider Fatima was expect-
ing, but upon Marvin, dangling from the rope. As they
watched, Marvin grunted, gave a mighty wrench with
all his might, and, with a loud tearing sound, split the
seam of his pants.

"You've got to be kidding me," Marvin said in a
weak and exasperated voice, just before he lost his grip

and plummeted through the air. He crashed into the hors d'oeuvre table, his impact upending it and showering him with dozens of appetizers as he rolled onto the floor. The punch bowl and all its contents arced overhead in a graceful, crimson-colored curve, a curve that ended directly atop Marvin's head with a roaring splash. The final casualty of his ill-fated flight was the life-size sculpture of Mr. Piggly Winks, which came sliding down the table. Marvin looked up just in time to see the plump belly of the anthropomorphic pig approaching his face. The force of the collision with fifty pounds of processed meat hurled him backward, and the head and limbs of the sculpture tore free and skittered across the floor.

The cafetorium broke out into riotous laughter. Little Stevie waded through the crowd, a smile on his face, and punched Fatima lightly in the shoulder. "That was a good one!"

"Ugh," Amber said, coming up beside him. "Disgraceful. Our moment of triumph has been tarnished by your klutzy cousin's butt."

Tilly Hoefecker glared at Fatima. "That girl will do anything for attention. Pathetic."

Gradually, they all turned away, leaving Fatima to stare, aghast, at Marvin's once-again-soggy figure. He shoved the broken body of Mr. Piggly Winks off to one side and turned his head toward Fatima.

"It's in the rafters!" he croaked. "It's got Lee!"

A look of grim determination settled over Fatima's face as she realized that there was just one thing left for her to do. She turned and marched across the room to where she could see a blurry red spot on the wall. It was a fire alarm. In one swift motion, she reached out with both hands and yanked down on the handle.

Immediately, two things happened. Alarms started screeching overhead, and a stream of blue dye shot out of a hidden nozzle on the fire alarm, straight into Fatima's face.

The kids shrieked at the sudden onset of the wailing sirens and the flashing strobes. "Fire!" the students screamed. Panic quickly set in.

"Outta my way!" Stevie said, pushing people out of his path. "God save the king!" He and Amber led the frightened stampede toward the doors, shoving aside chaperones, Mrs. Goudy, and the DJ, who vainly tried to instill some order before following the mob themselves. Within mere seconds, the dance floor was empty, save for Marvin, who clambered to his feet and brushed bits of finger food from his jacket, and Fatima, who sputtered as she wiped blue dye from her face.

"It was supposed to be an urban legend!" she said, rubbing her eyes. "It was supposed to be a scare tactic! No one *actually* puts blue dye into fire alarms!"

"Looks pretty blue to me," Marvin said, staggering over to her as he wiped Pork Punch from his own face.

Just then, Lee's voice cut through the wail of the sirens. "Help me!" he screamed. Marvin and Fatima looked up. There, lit by the flash of the emergency strobe lights, they could just make out the spider's huge bulk, and Lee's tiny shape struggling in the thing's clutches.

"We've got to do something!" Marvin said.

"How?" she said. "That thing took down an *elephant*! All we've got is a spork and a prayer! We're totally on our own here."

At that, the sound of a battle cry came from

outside, and the doors burst open. Ahab and Aristotle charged in, wearing kitchen aprons as armor and colanders and saucepans as helmets, and hauling their siege engine between them. Abraham brought up the rear a moment later, waving a wooden baseball bat and screaming, "We're here to save your soggy butt!"

"Never mind!" Fatima said. "It looks like we have some giant bugs on *our* side now!"

"We might have been better off on our own, actually," Marvin said under his breath. Then he had a realization. "Do those things work?" he asked, pointing to Ahab's wings as the big moth approached them. Another cry came from the rafters. "We need to get up there, now!"

Ahab scooped up Marvin in his arms, plunked him on his back between his wings, and took flight.

As anyone who has ever ridden on the back of a giant moth knows, there's only one good way to hang on. Marvin learned quickly, gripping the scruffy fur behind Ahab's wings as they spiraled upward. At last, Ahab alighted on the steel crossbeam where the spider perched, clutching Lee tightly to his abdomen.

Marvin had expected it would be hard to read the expression on a spider's face, but this one clearly seemed annoyed at having been interrupted. Still, he drew himself up into a regal pose, declaring, "Hail, oh mighty *Lepidoptera*! Have you come to face me, the great Caliban, in single combat?"

"Is he talking to you?" Marvin asked Ahab, still clinging to the moth's back. He peered past Ahab's bulk to get a better look at their foe. For a moment, he locked eyes with the captive Lee, whose pale brow was covered with beads of sweat.

"Don't interrupt your social betters, my clammy little friend," the spider said. "I prefer that my food remain silent when I eat it."

"Eat this!" Ahab shouted, lunging at the spider and swinging four different spatulas at the monster's head. The flurry of smacking utensils beat against the spider's face as though it were a snare drum, driving the creature backward. The moth continued to pound away at the spider until, backed up against the far wall, the monster finally lashed out in desperation.

Sharply jointed legs sliced through the air faster than the eye could follow, knocking the kitchen utensils from Ahab's grasp and sending him over onto his back. Marvin found himself half-pinned beneath the giant moth. They teetered on the edge of the beam. As Marvin struggled to wriggle free, he looked up to see the spider's seven remaining eyes looming over them.

"So easily disarmed," the spider said, shaking his head from side to side. "I, however, am never without *my* weapons." He reared up, exposing his fangs, which glistened with venom.

Marvin cast about desperately for some sort of defense. Ahab's spatulas were all gone, but in his apron—the can of nonstick Pork Spray. Marvin reached over and snatched it from the apron pocket, lifting it up just as the spider lunged forward.

A cone of meat-scented chemicals shot into the spider's remaining eyes. The monster reeled back in pain and clawed at his face with his many legs, dropping Lee in the process. Lee screamed in panic as he plunged through empty space.

Down on the gym floor, Aristotle, Abraham, and Fatima watched the struggle. Aristotle saw Lee plummeting to the ground and acted quickly to help: He shoved Abraham underneath him, using the moth's body to break the boy's fall.

"Oof!" Abraham said on impact. "Watch out! The Elephant Vampire's throwing humans at us!" He shoved Lee off him and took a look. "Oh, it's just the stinky boy."

"Gangway!" came a shout from above. Ahab and Marvin had seized the spider's moment of confusion and leaped from the beam. They spun toward the gym floor at a terrifying rate, but stopped at the last moment, Ahab drawing up into a graceful hover before touching lightly to the earth.

Marvin let go of Ahab's furry back and dropped to the floor. He reached down and helped Lee up to his feet.

"We're all safe," Marvin said, doing a quick head count. "Now let's get out of here!" Abraham and Ahab, Marvin, Fatima, and Lee all ran toward the exit.

"But, wait!" shouted Aristotle. "The coup de grâce! The triumph of Newtonian science over Shakespearean melodrama!"

The others stopped short of the door and looked back at the tall moth, who bustled around his siege engine in the middle of the gym floor.

"I don't know what he's talking about," said Abraham, "but this doesn't look good."

Aristotle plucked up the severed Pork Loaf head of the Mr. Piggly Winks sculpture and placed it in the basket of the catapult. Then he pulled an old barbecue lighter from his own battle apron and set the oily meat-head on fire.

"With this flame, I unseat the Bard!" he cried, and loosed the catapult.

The ball of burning meat shot up into the rafters like a greasy comet, catching the staggering spider squarely in the abdomen.

Aristotle shouted in triumph and danced in circles as the monster caught fire and fell back on the beam. Its legs flailed in the air as it tried to right itself and regain its balance. Flaming gobs of processed meat sprayed through the air and rained down on the cafetorium below, igniting the crepe paper streamers and spattering the walls and floor with small patches of greasy fire.

"My God!" Fatima said. "There's an actual fire now!"

"I guess that solves your problem of explaining the whole fire-alarm thing to the police," Marvin said.

"I was trying to save you!" Fatima said, wiping vainly at her blue cheeks.

"Really? Even after I hung you out to dry?"

"Yes, really!" Fatima said. "And after walking around with you and your soggy suit for an hour, I needed some drying time!"

"Look!" Lee shouted, pointing. The spider had tipped off the edge of the beam and was plummeting earthward—directly above Aristotle, who hadn't yet stopped dancing.

With a crash and a cry and a puff of smoke, the spider landed atop the moth.

The monster was still alive. And angrier than ever.

"You burnt my hair!" the spider growled, his face inches from Aristotle's startled compound eyes. "I'm going to shred you like pulled pork, and eat your guts with a plastic fork!"

"Th-th-that doesn't sound very d-dignified," Aristotle stammered.

"It was a rhyming couplet, you dolt!" the spider screamed. "Look it up!"

"Aristotle!" Ahab, said, and charged to his rescue. "Come on, everybody!"

Lee, his face flushed with anger, charged toward his former captor with a shout.

"I've got a new battle cry," Abraham said to Marvin. "Let me know if you like it." He ran to join the fight, screaming, *I regret meeting each and every one of you!*"

"I learned so little this year," Marvin said, "and now we're all going to die." He turned to Fatima. "Well, thanks for trying to save me earlier. Thanks for—for being my friend, I guess. And for being my first—and last—real date."

Fatima furrowed her brow, grabbed him by the head, and kissed him forcefully on the lips before running off to help the others.

Marvin stood frozen in place, utterly shocked. He didn't know whether his life was flashing before his eyes because he was about to die or what, but everything went quiet, and the events of the past few weeks began to uncoil in his memory. He had experienced what was arguably the worst first day of school anyone had ever had. He had occasionally mistreated those few individuals who had seen beyond his failings. Yet now, he found himself with friends. Real friends— friends he was willing to fight for. He stared blankly ahead like that for long moments, not moving, until the sounds of battle worked their way into his brain.

"Hey, Romeo!" Abraham shouted. "We could use a little help here!"

He looked up to see that, despite the onslaught of legs, wings, and fists, the fight was not going well for his side. Amid the flames and smoke, the spider struggled with Lee, who had leaped onto the monster's back and was beating on his massive head. Just as Ahab jumped up and flapped his wings to begin an aerial assault, the spider grabbed Lee and hurled him toward the giant moth. Ahab took the impact on his right wing, and it was torn to tatters, plunging both combatants to the ground with painful thuds.

Aristotle, meanwhile, had pulled himself free of the spider, but instead of fleeing or fighting hand-to-hand, he was busy trying to reload his siege engine. "I just need to recalibrate for a low-elevation target!" he said. Aristotle grabbed nearby scraps of Pork Loaf to refill the colander, then ignited them. But just as he moved the weapon into position, the spider broke loose and charged straight at him.

"Wait!" Aristotle cried. "I can't hit you if you're that close!" He backpedaled furiously, trying to get enough distance to launch his flaming payload—but in the process, he tripped and overturned the catapult on his head. The spider stopped and eyed Aristotle curiously as the moth struggled and yelped beneath the burning wreckage of his own machine.

"Oh no!" Fatima said. She ran to the wall and grabbed a fire extinguisher to put out the oily flames that now danced across the tall moth's hairy body. She sprayed white foam across him and the now-useless siege engine.

At this, the spider chuckled a little and performed the arachnid equivalent of a shrug. He turned back to see what was left of the rest of his foes—just in time to find himself face-to-face with Abraham.

"Time to call in the designated hitter!" Abraham bellowed, and, with a tight four-handed grip on his bat, swung with all his might. The bat connected with one of the spider's knees, and the spider shrieked in pain and fell to the floor. Abraham followed up with swing after swing to the beast's bloated abdomen. "You low-down insect wannabe!" Abraham said as he hammered away. "Grow a thorax!"

"Enough!" the spider grunted out between blows. "You irritate me with your blathering, so now I take your eye!"

"That doesn't make any sense!" Abraham protested.

"Here!" the spider said, and one of his limbs flashed out, striking at Abraham's left compound eye. The moth staggered backward, clutching his head.

The spider drew himself back up to his full height, upon which he heard a shout from behind. He turned and saw Fatima, her blue face glowering at the monster as she tightened her grip on the heavy fire extinguisher. "You are an unplanned-for contingency," she said, "and I HATE unplanned-for contingencies!" She spun around, swinging the metal canister behind her, and hurled it at the spider like an athlete performing the hammer throw.

The fire extinguisher sped past the spider, missing his head by inches and clattering uselessly to the floor. The spider hissed angrily at Fatima, who turned and ran.

Within seconds, the monster was upon her, and with a vicious swipe of his foreleg, he smacked Fatima across the midsection, hurling her sideways, across the room and into the wall. She came down hard on her bad leg.

"My knee!" she cried, huddling in a small heap on the floor.

"An eye for an eye," the spider said, gloating, as he glanced at Abraham, who had stumbled to the floor in pain, and then back to Fatima. "And a knee for a knee." The spider advanced slowly through the clouds of smoke toward Fatima, closing in for the kill.

Fatima's cries snapped Marvin out of his daze. As was his style, Marvin rushed forward without thinking, running to put himself between Fatima and the spider. On the way, he scooped up the only weapon he could find—the broken arm of the Mr. Piggly Winks statue. He skidded to a stop just in front of Fatima, and, wielding the Pork Loaf arm like some comic version of a hero's sword, took a swift swing at the head of the spider. The monster ducked the blow easily and stared at Marvin with surprise and amusement.

"You again!" the spider said. "We have some unfinished business, you soggy nuisance."

Despite the knee-shaking terror he felt, Marvin's innate sense of rudeness rallied, and he found himself talking back. "At least I'll dry off. I don't see your eye growing back anytime soon." Marvin thrust at the spider with the Pork Loaf arm. "Now scuttle out of here. Go back to whatever hole you crawled out of."

The spider chuckled. "Whatever hole I crawled out of?" he said. "You should know that place very well. It is the same dark pit of despair where you make your bed each night!"

"Shove it, you half-blind, smoldering hairball!" Marvin said, and swung ferociously at the spider's head. The spider grabbed the Pork Loaf arm out of Marvin's hands before the blow could connect, and casually tossed it away, far from Marvin's reach. Marvin swallowed nervously and took a step backward toward Fatima.

The spider laughed as he stepped forward. "You fool," he said, swinging his head from side to side, his eyes glittering in the flames that danced in patches across the gym floor. "Everything that has happened is your fault! All the pain and misery this town has endured. The broken bodies of your friends. And I, Caliban, who stand here to seal your doom. I owe my very existence to you—you and your faulty science! For it was your elixir that freed my great intellect to rule over you lesser creatures."

"How's that going for you?" Marvin asked, stepping backward. "Last I checked, you had been set on fire, lost an eye, and got your leg broke."

"Mock me all you want," the spider said. "It is *but sound and fury, signifying nothing*. Nothing can save you now." The spider edged forward and readied his fangs.

But he paused. He heard the clearing of a throat and looked back to see Lee holding the discarded Pork Loaf arm in one hand and smacking it against the palm of the other, like a billy club at the ready. "You miscalculated," Lee said.

"How's that?" the spider said.

"According to me and my friends' science experiment, six ounces of Pork Loaf, introduced to my digestive system, can generate enough force to take out an entire classroom," Lee said. He stared at Mr. Piggly Winks's arm as he hefted it. "How many ounces do you think *this* is?"

"Enough stalling, my little amuse-bouche," the spider said. "I tire of these games. I think the time has come for eating."

"I couldn't agree more," Lee said.

Marvin, realization slowly dawning, waved his hands in protest. "Lee, no—!"

Lee smiled and winked at Marvin.

Then he shoved the Pork Loaf arm into his mouth and began chomping.

19

The Seventh Smell

Since the dawning of the world, there have only been seven stenches so foul they left a mark on the very fabric of time and space. The first was the reek that rose from the primordial ooze, that stinking slop that covered the earth for millions of years and eventually belched forth upon the planet the first primitive forms of life. The second wave swept across the earth's surface sixty-five million years ago, when the bodies of countless dinosaurs rotted under the dark, ash-covered skies following a devastating meteor impact. It wasn't until 218 BC that one of the Great Odors was first experienced by human nostrils: The smell of Hannibal's forty-six thousand unwashed troops as they marched through the Alps behind a column of massive war elephants. The fourth smell was created by a Trappist monk who took a vow to set aside his cheese and refrain from eating it until he had finished transcribing his latest copy of the Bible; two years later, he retrieved the cheese from the monastery's cellar, unearthing the stinking forerunner of what would become Limburger. Years later, in Paris, the stink arising from the practice of throwing rubbish and waste directly into the streets was magnified tenfold on a particularly hot and windless summer afternoon to generate a smell so terrible, it drove the city's residents to madness and may have helped spark the French Revolution. In 1909, the sixth of the infamous odors led the organizers of the Boston Marathon to discontinue the celebratory tradition of tossing used gym socks into the Charles River after the race; the difficult river cleanup goes on to this day.

But nothing in the realm of human experience could prepare someone for the seventh smell. It shook heaven and earth, and seemed to bend the very air around Lee as it built up to full potency. Marvin knew it smelled bad, but it smelled *so* bad that he could no longer even call it a smell. It was an odor that was more felt than smelt, like a linebacker standing on your face. He also heard a hum, which started out so low he couldn't quite tell if it was there. Gradually, it increased in pitch, until it was reminiscent of the otherworldly chanting of throat-singing Buddhist monks.

When the sound grew high-pitched enough to become uncomfortable, Marvin saw objects begin to rise into the air.

First, plastic cups and paper plates lifted off from the tabletops and chairs where they had been set down. Then the chairs themselves began slowly skidding across the gym floor, their legs occasionally coming up off the ground before bouncing back down and skidding onward. Marvin felt himself being pulled sideways, and realized that everything in the room had begun churning in a clockwise circle, with Lee at its center. He, Fatima, the moths, and all the debris from the dance were being pulled across the floor or floated through the air in a sort of slow-motion cyclone.

"This is impossible!" screamed Aristotle over the keening sound. "The laws of physics do not allow for—"

"Can it!" shouted Abraham as he was swept along the floor beside Aristotle and the wreckage of his siege engine. "What do you know, bigmouth? You just got creamed by your own catapult!"

"Look out!" cried Ahab as he lost his grip on the floor and was hurled through the air and into the other two moths, his damaged wing flapping vainly against the unseen force. Ahab's giant, rotund body bowled over his compatriots and sent them all tumbling out the doors of the cafetorium and into the hallway.

The spider was scrabbling at the ground with his many limbs, desperately seeking purchase near the eye of the storm.

Marvin looked around for Fatima. She was swinging past a bit farther out from Lee, her feet barely touching the floor, her eyes wide with terror. "Give me your hand!" he said, and reached out for her. She groped frantically for his arm, missing several times before their fingertips touched and he pulled her in.

"Now what?" she asked.

"I don't know," Marvin said. "Do you have a page in your Harvest Dance binder for this?"

Fatima frowned at him. "Well, the tornado shelter is *supposed* to be the cafetorium!" she said. "I don't really know what you do when there's a tornado *in* the cafetorium!"

Fatima opened her mouth to say something else, but just then the force of the maelstrom spun them off into a corner of the room, wedging them against the wall and knocking the breath from their lungs. A long metal table followed soon after, turning over onto its edge and slamming against the walls on either side of them. It became wedged in place, trapping them in a small, triangular pocket of safety. They heard clang after clang as folding chairs piled up against the table like storm-tossed debris. When they recovered their senses, Marvin and Fatima clawed their way up and looked over the edge of the barricade.

In the center of the room, Lee stood motionless, his arms slack at his side. He had dropped the stub end of the Pork Loaf limb he had been eating, and his eyes were half-closed. Just in front of him, the giant spider continued to claw frantically at the ground, seeming almost to run in place as he fought the vortex. At last, Marvin saw the spider's hideous legs leave the ground, just as the noise reached an unbearably high, shrieking crescendo. The outline of Lee's body became indistinct, and Marvin realized that his friend was glowing brightly.

"Don't look at it!" Marvin shouted to Fatima, and they both ducked down behind the table.

With a flash of blinding white light, the world went silent.

The explosion was terrific. All the gym windows high overhead shattered outward. The flames that had licked the gym floor and walls were extinguished in an instant. Every remaining folding chair was flung hard against the walls in a perfect circle emanating outward from Lee. The metal table shielding Marvin and Fatima bent under the pressure but did not break.

The spider's body shot through the air and into the wall with tremendous force, leaving a disgusting green splat on the painted cinder blocks.

At last, Lee collapsed to the floor and was motionless.

Marvin and Fatima frantically dug their way out of the pile of chairs and tables. There was no sound as each crumpled folding chair clattered to the floor. They shouted to each other, but after the noise of the explosion, all they could hear was a high-pitched ringing. Marvin clambered over the mountain of metal and ran across the bare gym floor toward Lee's motionless body.

Lee's suit had been cut to ribbons by the force of the explosion, and tiny wisps of smoke rose from the charred edges of fabric. His light-blond hair was scorched in places, and his skin was pale and waxy.

Marvin couldn't tell if Lee was still breathing.

He bent over his friend and shook his body, shouting soundlessly into his ears.

A feeling of cold dread began to creep over Marvin's skin. At last, he realized it was not just fear, but actual cold—water was rushing past his ankles. He turned around and saw that the fire department had arrived, and they were blasting their hoses across the smoldering gym floor. Fatima was standing like a statue in a river, her blue dress rippling as the water flowed past her. The spider, amazingly enough, was gone. The flood was already washing away the trail of goo it had left behind when it fled out the doorway.

Marvin's concerns, however, were more immediate. As cold water surrounded him and soaked into his wrinkled wool pants, he silently mouthed, "Not again."

Lee opened his eyes and found himself standing. He was up to his knees in water, but unlike on the floor of the cafetorium, the water here was not cold. It was warm and soothing, and each gentle wave that washed past him seemed to take some of his cares away. He looked up and saw that he stood near the shore of a misty green island, and that figures waited for him on the sand. Some he could recognize, and some he could not, but they all seemed familiar, and they were all holding their noses.

Two of the figures waded out into the surf, and Lee realized they were his mother and father.

"Oh, Lee," his mother said, a sad smile on her face. "It's not time for you yet, honey. You need to go back."

"And quickly!" someone shouted from the shore.

"Shut up!" Lee's father said, turning back and glaring at the crowd. They all took a step back, shuffling their feet in the sand self-consciously.

"But, Mom—Dad," Lee said, his eyes filling with tears. "It's been so long."

"I know, honey," Lee's mom said, and she bent over and gave him a quick, firm hug before stepping back.

"But you still have a long way to go. Your friends need you right now."

Lee's father placed a strong hand on his shoulder and gave a squeeze. "Remember who your real friends are," he said. "We can see things in the world a bit differently from where we stand. We can see where you might end up. We don't want you falling in with the wrong people."

Lee opened his mouth to respond, but couldn't think of what to say. It was all too much, too fast. His mother smiled at him again, and his father spun him around firmly and pushed him out into the waves.

Lee went under the surface, and it seemed to him as though he was instantly plummeting down a waterfall.

Scenes from his life flashed past: running through the sprinkler on a hot summer day. Skinning his knee falling off a skateboard. Positioning green plastic army men for an epic battle on the living room rug. His mother shoving him up through the trapdoor of the tree fort and telling him to pull up the ladder behind him, and not make a sound. His father out on the lawn at night, shouting at people Lee couldn't see from his hiding place in the tree fort. The long walk up to his grandmother's house after his parents' funeral, his suit itching him uncomfortably, the house looking strange and unwelcoming. Day after day in school, held at more than arm's length by students and teachers alike. And lastly, those few short weeks spent with Marvin and Fatima, where he finally felt like he was being talked to and treated like a normal person.

And then he was on his back, and he was moving, and he heard a voice call out, "It smells like a burnt commode in there."

Lee opened his eyes and saw an EMT talking with a weary firefighter. They lifted his wheeled stretcher up into the back of an ambulance. "Probably cherry bombs in the toilet again," the firefighter said, then walked off to deal with the chaos of flashing lights and panicked people outside in the night.

"What a disappointment," Lee said. He turned his head sideways and saw Marvin sitting next to him, wrapped in a thick blanket.

"Well, it's good to have you back, anyway," Marvin said, and smiled.

Interlude

A dribbling trail of green goo marked a long and staggering path through the night, leading from the middle school toward the waterfront. The spider, nearly blind, kept banging into the walls of warehouses and the sides of steel cargo containers, muttering to himself all the while.

". . . but mark my words, you pathetic backwater of a town—I will survive this, and I will have my revenge! You will taste my venom, and I will leave you as nothing but withered husks!" He paused to cough, and looked down in alarm at the large pool of green fluid that was forming beneath him. "Oh, that's not good." He used two of his remaining limbs to hold together his wounded abdomen, and marched ahead on four legs. "Yes." He continued his rant. "Mark my words! My vengeance shall be swift and terrible!" He sighed, dropping his dramatic air for a moment. "Man, I'm tired. Where's that dockyard already?"

In time, the spider found himself at the water's edge. Stacks of crates and cargo containers towered about him on either side, and several cranes, used for unloading freight, loomed overhead. In the water, at the edge of the dock, floated a lone boat.

"Aha! A vessel!" the spider cried in relief. *"If the river were dry, I am able to fill it with my tears; if the wind were down, I could drive the boat with my sighs.* Time to ditch this stupid town." He started toward the gangplank.

"Hey, buddy," a voice called out coolly from the shadows.

"Hark!" the spider said, whirling about to face the interloper. "Who interrupts my exit grand, as I take to sea and quit the land?"

"Nice doggerel," the voice replied. "Been hitting the books pretty hard, haven't you?" A tall figure, wearing a long coat and an old-fashioned fedora, stepped into the dim light. It regarded the disfigured body of the spider, from broken limbs to scorched fur, with amusement. "I guess you're having a bad hair day, huh?

It looks like the gal at the beauty parlor set the curling irons to 'stun.'" He paused to sniff the air. "And the smell—kind of a mix of burning tires and porta-potty, wouldn't you say?"

The mysterious figure stood with his hands in the pockets of his trench coat. Two additional arms casually emerged from the open front of the coat and held a cigar and lighter up to his shadowed face. "You don't mind if I light up a little air freshener, do you? Of course you don't." He lit the cigar.

The spider was shaking in rage at all the indignities being hurled at him. "You have sealed your own doom, oh fedoraed one," the spider said. "You know not whom you have insulted!"

"Oh, I know exactly what you are," the figure said. He put his additional arms back inside his coat and took a long pull on his lighted cigar. "The question is, do *you*?"

"Of course I do," said the spider. "I am Caliban— mutant offspring of a Pork Punch taste test gone awry, and devoted disciple of the immortal Bard." Then he pulled himself up straighter, recalling his earlier dignity. "I am a superintelligent poetic killing machine. I am death on the wind." At this declaration, he bellowed and reared up before the figure in the trench coat, swinging two of his limbs into striking position and exposing his glistening fangs.

The figure shook his head from side to side, unimpressed by the spider's display. "Wrong," he said. "I'll tell you what you are. You're a liability. You're evidence that links back to PLI. And it's time to cut the cord."

He paused, clearly waiting for something to happen.

"I said, *it's time to cut the cord*," the figure repeated loudly. Again he paused, then turned to look to his left. "Cut the cord, dimwit!"

A smaller figure poked its head out from the shadows. "Sorry, boss—I don't have any fingers."

"Give me that," said the tall figure, grabbing a long, taut rope and slicing it in two with a sudden, fast motion.

The spider heard the furious squealing of a pulley wheel overhead, and looked up just in time to see a giant wooden shipping crate come crashing down upon him.

The tall figure let out a long sigh and stepped forward to examine his work. He pulled off his fedora, revealing the angular, alien features of a praying mantis. He pointed to the side of the crate, where the words "Contents: Boots" were stenciled across the wood.

"Stomped him, eh?" he said to his short companion. "Nice touch. That's poetic justice, right there."

His companion stepped fully into the light, revealing the form of a squat, three-foot-tall cockroach. "Thanks, boss."

The mantis pulled a mobile phone from its coat and dialed a number. "Yeah, you know that thing you wanted me to take care of?" he said to the listener on the other end of the call. "No, no, the other thing. The BIG thing. That thing with the legs and all the slaughter . . . right. Well I made the 'delivery,' if you know what I mean. And it killed him. What? No. I'm telling you I dropped a giant crate on top of his head. Yeah. Okay. Good-bye."

He hung up and stowed the phone away again. "Come on, Francis," he said to his sidekick. "Let's go get a nice hot cup of soup."

"Yeah, I'm starving," the roach said.

As the two left the pier, a white van marked with the words "Big Pest Exterminators" pulled up beside the smashed crate. Men in yellow hazmat suits climbed out, pulling long vacuum hoses behind them, and immediately got to work. By morning, there'd be no sign left of any spider, superintelligent or otherwise.

20

The Highest Honor

In most stories, something good happens to everyone at the end. This story is no exception.

The emergency room doctor who treated Lee's injuries after the dance told Lee's grandmother that, judging by the condition of the boy's skin and the fact that he had eaten so much Pork Loaf that evening, Lee might be allergic to something in the processed-meat product and should probably avoid it. Which meant that, once he recovered and all the Pork Loaf worked its way out of his system, Lee no longer smelled. So that was good. Unfortunately, that didn't change the fact that no one at school liked him. Still, Lee was content in the knowledge that he had saved the lives of Marvin and Fatima, and probably the rest of Butcherville—even if hardly anyone knew it. And as his father had told him—had that been his father? It all seemed so hazy now—while it mattered that he had friends, who those friends were mattered more.

Fatima, seemingly caught red-handed—and blue-faced—received a week of in-school suspension. Everyone accused her of pulling the fire alarm in order to spoil Stevie and Amber's moment as Harvest King and Queen. In addition to her suspension, Fatima was required to speak with the school counselor once a week in order to deal with her "issues." As it turned out, this wasn't all bad. She got a lot of things off her chest, and realized that her life would be less stressful and she would be happier if she didn't try to control everything that went on around her. Fatima also winnowed her collection of portable devices down to a single all-in-one smartphone, so despite the fact that her knee brace was now larger and more menacing than ever, she was able to walk down the hall looking like a normal kid, rather than the sample counter at an electronics store.

Little Stevie Upton basked in the afterglow of his Harvest coronation. Even though he had knocked down a dozen people while fleeing the school, he was able to spin it afterward to sound like he was, in fact, a hero, blazing a trail amid the confusion so that others might follow him to safety. He became more popular than ever. This just goes to show that good things happen to bad people, and good things happen to good people, and good things happen to people who are not particularly good or bad.

As for Marvin, in spite of everything that had happened to *him*, he went home to find he was still living in the attic.

That night, after the dance, Marvin changed out of his wet clothes and into some flannel pajamas. He tried to straighten up his room, and started by undoing the damage to his bed and dresser that the moths had caused.

As he was making his bed, he heard a knock at the door. "Marvin? Sweetie?" his mom called, opening the door. "Finally dried off? I know it can get cold up here, so I wanted to make sure you didn't catch a chill." She handed him a thick wool blanket. "I figured you could use an extra blanket."

"Thanks, Mom," Marvin said. He spread the

blanket out on his bed, and got under the covers. His mom sat down on the edge of his mattress.

"I know it probably hasn't been easy for you these past few months," she said. "A new baby in the house, having to give up your room—and all while starting middle school." Marvin didn't say anything.

"How is school?" she asked. "Things are going okay there?"

Marvin shrugged. "Apart from the explosions, you mean?"

His mom laughed. "It does feel that way sometimes, doesn't it?" she said. "Well, listen. I just want you to know that you're still an important part of this family, even if you're all the way up here. You're still under our roof. And you can come to your father or me for anything. We're always here for you."

"Thanks, Mom," Marvin said. She leaned over and gave him a hug. Just then, Baby Harry began to wail downstairs. Marvin's mom sighed, and stood up to go.

"We should really get your father to do something about these bare walls and rafters," she said, looking around at the attic. "Some drywall, some paint—"

"Some insulation," Marvin said.

"Exactly," his mom said, nodding. "I'll have him get to work on it tomorrow." She headed out the door. "Good night, sweetie," she said.

"Good night, Mom."

"And, honey," she said as she was closing the door, "you should really try to keep your room a little neater. It looks like a war zone in here."

Marvin settled back against his pillows and tried to relax. The sound of Baby Harry's crying gradually subsided downstairs. Marvin could tell his mom had been feeling guilty for paying so little attention to him these past few weeks, but he hadn't much felt like talking. He had just survived the single most stressful evening of his life—one that made even his first day of school seem harmless—and he was exhausted. And even if he wanted to, he couldn't begin to figure out how to talk to his mom about the moths, the spider, or Lee and his strange power.

Just then, he heard some muffled voices nearby and noticed that his dresser, which he had reassembled and shoved up against the wall to hide the giant hole from his mom, had started quivering. Finally, with a loud grunt and a cry of "Heave!" the dresser toppled over and Abraham climbed through the hole in the wall.

"Some idiot covered up this opening with a dresser," said Abraham, dusting some loose bits of wood and plaster from his furry body. "Don't you people over here know that you can't block the egress? It's a fire hazard."

Aristotle clambered out next. He was wrapped head to toe in gauze bandages, and reeked of scorched hair and various medicinal unguents. He stepped forward unsteadily and bumped into Abraham.

"Hey, watch it!" Abraham said. "Geez, you look and smell like a poorly embalmed mummy," he said to Aristotle.

"I'm sorry," the tall moth said, adjusting the bandages around his head. "The gauze keeps slipping down over my eyes. Plus, I've been completely coated in benzocaine, so I'm afraid I don't have a sense of touch at the moment."

Ahab emerged last and waved sheepishly to Marvin.

"How's the wing?" Marvin asked.

Ahab flexed his damaged right wing. The hole in it had been hastily patched with duct tape. "Good as new," he said.

"Well," Abraham said, "before we move on to bigger and better things, I'd just like to tell you that this establishment you run is subpar. Additionally, here." He threw a cardboard box to the floor. "Some of your hideous junk that we accidentally took when we moved out. I can't stand the sight of it. Especially since I now only have one eye. And, might I add, I still await your APOLOGY for gross slander and wrongful accusations against my person for Elephant Vampirosity in the third degree."

Aristotle smacked the short moth in the back of the head, causing Abraham to grunt in protest and adjust the patch that now covered his left compound eye.

"Did you just ask me to apologize to you in the middle of *your* apology for stealing my stuff?" Marvin asked.

"He is the M.C. Escher of logic," Aristotle said.

"Be that as it may," Abraham said, clearing his throat loudly, "it has been brought to my attention by others who were there that you are partially responsible for our survival. Therefore, it is my privilege—and I use the term loosely—to bestow upon you this, our highest honor, with liberty and justice for all."

Abraham leaned over and draped a medal around Marvin's neck.

Marvin lifted the medal and examined it. "Third place in the 2010 Recycolympics?" he asked.

"No, no, no," Ahab said, reaching out to turn the medal over. "The other side."

On the reverse, the moths had crudely carved the words "GOOD JOB" into the copper-colored plastic disc.

"It is an award for exceptional bravery under fire," Aristotle said.

"Did you just find this in one of the attics?" Marvin asked.

" 'Find' is an interesting word . . ." Aristotle said, trailing off into silence.

"Okay," Abraham said at last. "I know we've been evicted from the premises. Don't think that's gone unnoticed. Come on, boys. We missed the ball game tonight while we were saving someone's soggy little hide at the school gym, but maybe we can still catch the highlights." He and the other moths turned to go.

Marvin sighed. "Wait," he called out. The moths

stopped and turned back a little too quickly. They stared at him expectantly.

Marvin thought for a moment. Yes, they were insulting. They were selfish. They were hideous-looking. But they had come to the rescue. And their being around did make the attic a less lonely place.

"You guys can stay and hang out for a little bit, if you want," Marvin said. "I don't have a TV, though."

"No problem!" Abraham said. The three moths disappeared quickly through the hole in the wall, and reemerged with various-size TV sets in their various-size arms. They quickly reconnected the stolen cable and tuned the sets to different stations to watch the baseball highlights on the late news shows.

"Make yourselves at home," Marvin said as the moths sprawled about the room. Ahab settled himself at the foot of Marvin's bed.

"You gonna eat that?" the giant said, eyeing Marvin's new blanket and smacking his mandibles hungrily. Marvin thought for a moment, then reached over to his desk for a pair of scissors. He cut the blanket in half down the middle, giving a piece to the delighted moth.

Marvin curled up in bed, bathed in the bluish glow of sports replays and surrounded by the sounds of muttering moths and the soggy chewing of wool fibers. And as he drifted off to sleep in his half blanket, Marvin realized that friendship came in many shapes and sizes. Some friends were a little smelly. Some friends were a little bossy. And some friends had more arms than usual. They might be strange, but they were still friends. And that would just have to do.

Epilogue

Stephen Upton Sr. concluded the PLI annual shareholders meeting on a high note. "Thanks to our retooled online distribution-tracking system, we've seen a five percent growth in orders and a corresponding drop in the costs of shipping and fulfillment." He paused in his speech, sneaking a glance at his watch as the applause in the boardroom swelled and then died down. "And I'd like to offer a special tip of the hat to our science team, which has increased the nutritional quality of Pork Loaf by one point five percent during the past fiscal year, well ahead of our projections and far in advance of government guidelines. I think we can all agree, the future looks bright indeed for Pork Loaf International." Again, the boardroom erupted into applause, and Stephen adjourned the meeting, exiting the room quickly by way of a small door at the rear.

He took the freight elevator down to the basement

garage, where a large black Humvee waited. He climbed in, and the driver headed out of the building and off the carefully manicured grounds of the PLI corporate campus.

As the sun sank toward the western horizon, the Humvee wound its way through rolling hills and bare autumn trees, at last pulling up to the drive of the Butcherville Country Club. A guard opened the gates and waved it through, and the vehicle drove up to the front steps of the clubhouse just as the sun was setting behind the eighteenth hole of the golf course.

"Good afternoon, sir," said the valet as he opened the door. "Meeting someone for cocktails?"

"Something like that," Stephen Upton said, and he grabbed his briefcase and strode up the steps, walking across the oak-paneled lobby to an elevator. Once the doors closed, he removed from his pocket a large brass key shaped like an elephant's head, then inserted its trunk into a keyhole on the control panel and twisted. A soft chime rang out, and the elevator began descending. It passed the billiards room. It passed the locker rooms. It passed the basement utility rooms and kept going, even though there were no more floors marked on the display. At last, the elevator stopped, and the doors opened onto a narrow, dimly lit hallway. Stephen walked down the corridor, through a nondescript door, and into a blacked-out room. He was expected.

"That was a fine performance this evening, Stephen," a voice called out from the dark. A television screen on the wall cast a faint light over the room, revealing dim figures seated around a long table. The TV screen showed a live video feed of the PLI boardroom, where the last attendees of the shareholders meeting were filing from the room. "I couldn't have done it better myself."

"You did do it better yourself," another voice called out. "I remember."

"Did I?" said the first speaker. "I may have, and I may not have."

"Oh, drop the pretense," said the second man. "I know who you are."

"Do you?" replied the first. "I don't know any of you, and you don't know me. That's what we agreed to—what our founders agreed to."

"Come now. We've each guessed one another's identities long ago. We're all friends here."

"Friends?" replied the first speaker, swiveling in his chair. "Are we? I thought we were here to shape the destiny of the most important corporation in the world. That doesn't sound like a friendly get-together to me." His chair creaked as he turned back toward the door. "In fact, we're here today because we have a dangerous situation on our hands. Stephen? Will you brief the assembly?"

"Very well," said Stephen. He nervously straightened his tie. These meetings always made him uncomfortable, and never more so than when he had to share bad news. "The autopsy has confirmed that the spider was one of ours." A murmur passed around the table.

"Can it be traced back to us?" another man asked.

"Absolutely not," Stephen promised. "Once our special operative neutralized the threat, a cleaning team stepped in to remove all evidence of the, uh, 'Elephant Vampire.'"

"'Elephant Vampire,'" echoed the second speaker. "That was risky, Stephen, feeding that cover story to the police and the press. I can't believe they went for it. Good thing it worked."

"Yes, sir," Stephen said. "But . . . I'm afraid there is more news."

"More?" said the first speaker. "Continue, Stephen."

"The evidence retrieved following the uh, incident, at the middle school," Stephen said, "points to the involvement of not one, but *four* bogeys."

"What?" sputtered one of the men. "Four? What evidence?"

"There were unreliable eyewitness accounts of several 'moth-men' fleeing from the scene," said Stephen. He paused and swallowed hard. "And we retrieved a portion of a wing."

Everyone at the table immediately began arguing and leveling accusations of incompetence. Finally, the first speaker stood up.

"Gentlemen. Please." The room quieted. He turned toward Stephen. "This is most serious," the speaker said. "Additional bogeys are a problem, and the flying ones . . . they're often unpredictable. Hard to track." Murmurs of agreement sounded from around the table. "Furthermore," he continued, "this indicates the involvement of a rogue agent using material from *our* labs for his own mysterious purpose. One bogey might be an accident, but four . . ."

"Our—our thoughts exactly, sir," Stephen stammered.

"Well, Stephen," the first speaker said, "it appears you have your work cut out for you. I hope you're up to the task." He waved his hand in dismissal and sat back down with a creak.

Stephen nodded nervously, and picked up his briefcase with clammy hands.

"We expect your next report to be . . . more favorable," said the speaker. "And Stephen—" He paused. Stephen turned in the doorway and looked back. "You should try the prime rib up in the clubhouse restaurant. It's excellent tonight."

Stephen nodded again and left the room quickly. In the pale glow of the lone television screen, eleven faces stared after him, all of them wearing elephant masks.

ACKNOWLEDGMENTS

This ridiculous book took more than ten years to put together. It would not have been possible without a lot of assistance. Thank you to our agent, Jill Grinberg, for entertaining our insectoid dreams on this long journey. Thanks to Matt's sister, Jenni, for the encouragement. Thanks to Shana Corey for early editorial advice. Thanks to Nick Eliopulos for getting the joke. Thanks to Google Docs for making our long-distance collaboration possible. And, of course, thanks to our wives for putting up with our many phone calls and our loud, confusing laughter during the writing of this book.

ACKNOWLEDGMENTS

ABOUT THE AUTHORS

Matthew Holm and Jonathan Follett met in middle school, where they started a rock band that rarely left Matt's basement.

Many years later, they're still close friends (and not entirely recovered from the traumas of middle school). Matt is an award-winning illustrator and frequent collaborator with his sister, Jennifer L. Holm, on graphic novels like the *New York Times* bestseller *Sunny Side Up* and the Babymouse and Squish series. Jon is a user experience designer and an internationally published expert on information design and emerging technologies.

Despite living on separate coasts, Matt and Jon still collaborate on creative projects together, proving that the bonds forged in middle school can never be broken.